Council of Worlds Universe

Brenna

Lyons

Wolkin: Mellaia

Book One

PUBLISHER

Chapter One

Grom raised his head, catching the wind on his cheek, feeling more wariken than man. What was it about this world that affected him so remarkably?

No. It wasn't just him. Whatever it was affected them all. His ordered band of conquerors were drunk on the rays of this little moon and restless as buck adolescents scenting their first female.

Female. The scent came to him again. Dear Monnan, the smell was divine. His soul cried out for her, even as his mind argued that she wasn't Wolkin, that the heir to Wolkin could not take a mate incapable of carrying his seed.

Her scent called him misguided. She was near-fertile, and she was the right female for Grom. Monnan, but her smell alone was enough to lure him to her. He advanced on her, following the tang of her body.

Bevor, his captain, came to Grom's side. He raised his head, drawing in her scent. A low growl rumbled up from his chest, and the captain tensed.

Grom turned on him and grasped Bevor by the throat in warning. Talking himself away of taking wariken form and ripping the other man's throat out was more difficult than he wanted to admit. For a long moment, they stared at each other. Then Bevor averted his gaze.

That took the edge off Grom's fury. "No one touches her but me," he ordered softly.

"Yes, my prince." Bevor's voice was little more than a gasp of air.

Mollified by his agreement, Grom released him and went back to his track. With every step closer to her, he wanted her more.

And then he saw her. She was a lush, breathing reproduction of the Goddess Dame herself, clad only in a diaphanous gown that reached her knees. The moon she danced beneath shimmered on black hair with deep red lights of color that fanned out around her undulating body. The triangle of her feminine curls and the caps of her dark nipples appeared and disappeared in the swish of fabric and hair.

Her dance was one of seduction, but there was no male about to be drawn by it but Grom. It was one of longing, and he didn't doubt what she longed for. It was a mating dance unlike any he'd seen before.

The dance did its work well. His cock rose to its full length. His body burned in want, fueled by the instinctive need all bucks both craved and despised.

No buck relinquishes his solitude easily.

Oh, but he would relinquish it to this little temptress. One look at the way the seductress moved her hips made it clear to him that she would taste his full length while their moon was high.

Grom motioned to Bevor to keep his men back, then strode into the clearing. He stopped as she did, staring into her pale blue eyes.

He waited for her reaction to his presence here. Would she invite his approach or would she run or fight? No matter the case, she would be his. If she ran or fought, his wariken would revel in the chase. If she invited him, it would be a sweeter mating.

Her gaze didn't shift to take his measure. Slowly, as if in acceptance of his unspoken claim on her, her hips began to sway in her mating dance again. Grom stepped toward her and a gasp escaped her lungs. She didn't flee; instead, her dance took on a more potent edge.

When he was less than a hand away, she rose on her bare feet, her swiveling hips taunting his ready length as their mouths meshed. Her small, warm hands trailed up his chest, delving beneath the bright-colored vest that announced his station. Grom shrugged it off and let it fall to the soft grass. His mate wanted him unclothed, and he would deny her nothing within reason. He might even grant her a few unreasonable things, if it pleased her.

The moon beat down on him fully, making the wariken within wild for her. Grom released his soft tied trousers and let them slip down his legs to pool around his ankles. His mate moaned into his mouth at the change, and his patience snapped.

Grom ripped his mouth from hers, steadying her as she toppled toward him. An oath to Monnan whispered from between his lips, and Grom cursed his shaking hands silently. He was a Wolkin prince. What madness was it that he was trembling in this woman's arms?

I must have what is mine. Any female who can make me tremble is my equal.

He grasped her shoulders and turned her, so her back faced him. She slipped a little and landed on the flats of her feet, bringing the top of her head to the center of his chest. Still, she didn't run from him. Grom forced her to her knees and dropped to his own behind her.

She started moving again, the soft material covering her buttocks stroking circles over his cock, enflaming him. He joined in the dance, touching her intimately, until little moans of pleasure escaped her. Words in her language whispered from her, some plea he couldn't understand.

I understand her well enough. Grom dragged the gown to the small of her back with one hand and forced her shoulders down with the other. Her luscious ass came up as her shoulders went down, and Grom thrust inside her heated channel, savoring the feeling of her female barrier tearing at his advance, at the sharp intake of breath and tensing of muscles that announced her pain.

She didn't pull away from the pain as he'd been led to believe females usually did their first time. Grom soothed her all the same. She whispered more words in that same pleading tone. Though he couldn't understand her language, the grinding movements of her core against his cock were impossible to misunderstand.

He gave himself over to the mating, setting a pace as old as time. Soft cries of pleasure escaped her mouth, sounds that announced her contentment with her place as his mate. As if confirming it, whispers of her climax taunted him.

Taking his cue to heart, Grom bit down on her shoulder. He growled as she screamed, and climax rushed through both of them. Monnan, but her blood was like fine spice on the tongue. His head spun, his body emptying into his mate. His cock swelled to lock him inside her body, and stillness descended on his soul. Grom bathed her mating wound, soothing her shivering and the whimpers of pain from his mate.

Shouts rose around him, and Grom wrapped her in his arms, abruptly aware that he had no hope of protecting her while he lay locked in her body. *I should have taken her further away from the settlement. I should have considered that her screams would alert the males of her species.*

A chorus of growling and snapping heralded the coming battle. The deadly Wolkin conquerors would defend their foolish prince and his mate with their lives.

Thank the Goddess.

His mate stiffened as the screaming started. She shook her head, and what were surely her protests rivaled the sounds of battle. Grom's mind worked quickly. These males were her family and her townspeople. They were here to protect her.

My mate wishes them unharmed. "Let them live, if you can," he bellowed.

In the distance, he heard his command being passed in the language of the wariken.

His mate trembled in his arms, and a tear wound down her cheek. Grom wiped it away, whispering soothing sounds. He tried to shield her view of the battle, but she probably saw too much.

His cock lessened, and Grom slid from her body. He donned his trousers and fastened them over his blood and semen-soaked length. She didn't try to escape him, as he feared she might. Instead, she sank to the grass, seemingly shocked.

The sounds of fighting tapered off to the moans of the injured. Rustling in the treeline let him know his soldiers were resuming man forms and donning clothing abandoned while they fought as wariken.

Grom snatched up his vest, intent on pulling it on, then glanced at his mate. His men had seen too much of her already.

He turned her in his arms and slid the vest over her gown to cover her breasts.

Her pale blue eyes held questions, begging answers he had no common language to give her. Instead, he touched his chest, growling his name. When she didn't answer in kind, Grom repeated the move, then touched her cheek, inviting her to gift him the name of his mate.

"Mellaia," she whispered. Her eyes fluttered, then shut.

"Mellaia," he repeated the strange sounds. Grom lifted her into his arms, then looked at the destruction around them. His heart sank at the truth. If they stayed here, there would be more battles. For Mellaia's sake, he had to take her away.

* * * *

Mellaia swallowed hard, her body hot and aching, trying to piece together what had happened to her. She'd performed the dance her grandmother had taught her, the ancient moon magic that would call the perfect man to her.

The raw need and pain inside brought memories of the man Luna had summoned, a man wholly unlike any she'd seen before. Disturbing memories of wolves and men at war made her head spin.

Heat and the potent smell of male musk were her only indications that Grom was near. Then his lips touched hers, and Mellaia turned to him fully, needing him despite the lingering aches of his first possession.

He whipped the bed coverings away, leaving her exposed to him. His mouth and hands explored her, tasting her pebbled nipples, the flat plane of her stomach, and then her center. Mellaia cried out harshly and forced her eyes open.

His hair was black as night, unbound so the silken locks caressed her inner thighs as he made love to her with his tongue. She arched up, pleading for him to make her his again.

Grom came up over her with a growl, his golden eyes locked on hers. His cock slid deep inside her, and Mellaia grasped at his broad shoulders.

Dear Luna, she'd never dreamed a man could feel so good. No wonder her grandmother told her there was magic in finding the mate Luna intended for you.

He thrust again and again, speaking in his guttural language. The tones were soothing ones, at odds with his fierce expression. "Mellaia." He said her name, over and over, a mantra that sped as his movements did likewise.

She replied with his name, at a loss for anything else he would understand.

He roared, his seed massaging her tender tissues. Her scant memories of their first loving gave her only a moment's warning before his cock swelled within her. Grom forced her hips to his bed when she moved to buck him off. He stroked her body, enticing her muscles to unknot. At last, he lessened, but he lay inside her, softening slowly.

Mellaia sighed, feeling oddly comforted. Though his lovemaking was unnatural, she knew she would never respond to another now that she'd known Grom's touch.

* * * *

Grom smiled as her breathing slowed and became deep and even. Her eyes slid shut, and her hand trailed lazily from his hip to the mattress. Still, he held himself inside her, going flaccid inside his sleeping mate.

7

Monnan, but he hadn't meant to succumb to her charms again so soon. She was simply so responsive to him that he couldn't help himself.

His cock slipped from her body, and Grom eased away and covered her with the quilts. Mellaia would wake again soon. Hunger and bodily needs would surely force her from sleep.

When she did, he would have to care for her and see to her needs. Grom would also have to learn to communicate with her. For that, he would have to train the translator unit to her language.

Mellaia sighed, then curled to her side beneath the quilt. The mating bite he'd left was an angry red and swollen. Grom touched it, wincing at the heat it radiated. It was unusual for the bite to become infected, but he would have to treat it carefully and watch for signs of it. After all, Mellaia was his mate.

Chapter Two

The smell of roasted meat prompted a deep grumble from Mellaia's stomach. She opened her eyes, seeking out the platter of food Grom held.

He stood by the side of the bed, nude and semi-erect. Mellaia tried not to stare, but she hadn't had a chance to see Grom fully yet. He was even more imposing in the nude than he'd been dressed and standing beneath Luna's light.

Food. I should eat something. She directed her gaze at the platter. Her cheeks flamed to life, as she recognized Grom's knowing smile.

He didn't give her time to be embarrassed. Instead, he slid to the bed next to her and laid the platter on his crossed legs. Grom plucked a cube of meat off the platter and brought it to her lips. "Maddae," he whispered.

Mellaia opened her mouth to take the meat, but he pulled it away, shaking his head.

Grom lifted the platter of food with one hand. With the other, he pointed to the meat. "Maddae." Then to the bread. "Tanta." Then to the fruit. "Suct."

Mellaia nodded, trying to commit the words to memory. "Maddae," she requested.

Again, he shook his head. He pointed to the meat again. "Maddae." He stared at her, patiently waiting for something.

I didn't pronounce it wrong. Maybe he wants to learn my language as well. "Maddae. Meat.'

He smiled widely, then offered a cube of the meat for her to eat. Grom waited until she swallowed, then pointed to the bread. "Tanta."

"Tanta. Bread. Suct. Fruit."

9

Grom laughed heartily and laid the platter on her lap. Mellaia took another cube of meat, savoring the succulent treat. She pointed to the platter, waiting for his response. There were hundreds of questions she had for him, but they needed communication to accomplish the task.

"Dek," he informed her.

"Dek, platter."

He leaned across the platter and kissed her.

Mellaia felt it hard to breathe. "Kiss." She brushed her lips across his to demonstrate, and repeated the word for him.

"Seg, kiss," he grumbled. Grom moved away abruptly, motioning to the platter of food.

Mellaia took another bite, but there was a more pressing concern. *And no way to ask for it properly.* She fidgeted, trying to find a way to explain her needs to him.

Grom placed his fingertips under her chin and guided her face up. He stared at her, seemingly questioning what had her so distracted. His eyes widened a bit, and he jumped from the bed and offered his hand to help her up. Mellaia went with him, hoping he understood what she needed, that he'd somehow guessed that a person, upon waking, would need to relieve their bowls and bladder.

The small room attached to the one containing the bed had three heavy pieces of furnishing. The largest looked like an empty pond. The second was taller and looked like a bowl set into a small table, likewise empty. The final was akin to a chair, but there was a bowl set into it, and the bowl had a small amount of water in it. Mellaia shot Grom a questioning look.

As if he understood her concern, he relieved himself into the bowl of the chair and pushed a button that made the water rush away. Mellaia didn't question him. She settled on the chair and emptied her bladder in a rush. Before she could press the button to send the foul water away, Grom knelt before her and used a damp cloth to bathe between her legs. He deposited it in the water, then used a second to clean the bloody leavings of their first mating from her inner thighs. At last, he pushed the button, and helped her to her feet.

He pointed to the seat. "Tesh." Then he took her to the empty bowl and raised a lever that filled it with warm water. "Tenha." A second lever released the water.

Mellaia rushed ahead of him to the pond and found a similar lever system to start water flowing, to block the flow, and to release it when she wished to.

Grom watched her explore, a faint smile on his face. He motioned to the pond. "Tempha."

Mellaia pointed to the first. "Tess."

"Tesh," he corrected her gently.

She nodded. "Tesh." She shook her head to indicate that she had no word to teach him for it.

Grom nodded and waved her on.

She pointed to the bowl set in the table. "Tenha." Again, she shook her head. Finally, she pointed to the last. "Tempha. Pond."

He smiled and led her back to the bed. Mellaia ate ravenously, but the question of how long it had been since her last meal was as unanswerable as thousands of others. When she'd had her fill, she handed the platter back to Grom. He set it aside without sampling any of the food, making her wonder if he'd eaten while she slept.

"Tesh?" he offered.

Mellaia shook her head.

"Tempha?"

"Yes."

He cocked his head to one side.

She nodded and hurried to her feet. Grom rose and stepped between her and the room. Mellaia looked up at him, uncertain.

He nodded. "Vit. Yes." Then he shook his head. "Prow. No."

"Vit. Tempha."

He smiled again and guided her to the pond. Grom demonstrated how she could change the water's temperature by rotating the lever. It was a wondrous system, and she marveled at the magic of it.

He offered three scented blocks of what she assumed were soaps and let Mellaia choose the one she liked best from them. Though Grom didn't touch her while she bathed, he watched her, his expression promising delights at a later time.

By the end of her bathing, it was all she could do to concentrate on the seemingly endless words Grom presented for her to learn. When they'd extinguished all of the furnishings in the room, he showed her an amazing box that magically showed realistic recreations of thousands of plants, animals, places, people, and situations.

Several times, she tried to beg off or question him, only to be directed back to the task. It seemed meaningless to her. Mellaia could scarcely remember a handful of the words Grom used in the hours they traded language. It hardly seemed possible he could remember more than she did. Moreover, he wasn't taking breaks to test her knowledge of the words. Once he'd matched a word to an image, he moved along and never returned.

At last, Grom lifted her in his arms and carried her to the bed. Solemnly, he catalogued the many words for her body, starting with her toes, fingers, and hair, then moving steadily inward from there. His hands became more intimate with every word they traded.

His mouth joined in the exploration, and he requested the words for lips, teeth, and tongue between increasingly heated kisses. Mellaia's concerns melted away. She gave him words for shoulders, breasts, nipples, abdomen, buttocks, and — finally — her aching clit and sheath. His circling fingers had her gasping for breath, praying to Luna the language lesson was over.

Almost over. Mellaia encircled his cock with her hand. She stroked, pleading silently for one more word.

"Peget," he grumbled.

"Cock," she whispered in return.

Grom growled out both words. Then he eased away from her, lifted his hand, and removed wide cuff from his ear. He separated it into two smaller cuffs, placed one back on his own ear, then attached the other to her ear.

Mellaia touched it, confused. What was the meaning of this? Did it mark her as Grom's? If so, why wait until now to give it to her?

He placed his fingertips across her forehead and smoothed them down, prompting her to close her eyes. Grom spoke softly in his language, and a moment later, his voice echoed into the ear with the cuff on it...in hers.

"Hear my words, Mellaia?"

She gasped. "Yes. What magic is this?"

"Magic?" he asked. No word emerged from the cuff. Obviously not every word translated. That was why his question sounded so stilted.

"How do you do this thing? Is it a gift from your gods?"

He chuckled, a dark sound of seduction. "Gods offer this?"

Mellaia opened her eyes, taking his measure. Did he not believe in the gods? "If Luna brought you to me, why could one of the others not supply a way for us to speak?" *Or the other wonders she'd seen, for that matter? Hot water that required no fire, water emerging from solid walls...*

Grom's smile melted into a look of wonder. "You praise Luna?" But Luna didn't emerge from his own lips. It was another name. Monnan.

The odd separation of his lips' movements and the words she understood made her head spin. "Of course. Do you not?"

"Night and day. You...she brought me to you?"

Mellaia didn't doubt something had been lost there.

"You praise she brought me to you?"

"That was the intent of my dance. It is an ancient magic, passed mother to daughter, Luna to her first daughter on Earth and then down through the line of healers."

"Dance is a prayer to Luna?"

She nodded. "For the man she intends as my mate."

His lips brushed hers, light as the flutter of a young bird's wings.

"What is it?" she asked.

"You are my mate. You pray to Luna for me. She brought me to you."

Chapter Three

Four days later

Grom snapped awake, aware only of the heat radiating off of Mellaia's body and soft cries escaping her lips. He touched her face, then launched from the bed, through the door, and into the corridor, with barely a pause to code the door open on the way.

A young soldier from a distant cousin's line gaped in wide-mouthed shock at Grom's nudity in the public spaces of the ship. He regained his composure quickly enough, when Grom ordered him to fetch Bevor. The young one had barely turned to run when Grom returned to his mate's side, a damp cloth in hand to bathe her face.

The captain was more a battle surgeon than a proper healer, but infection of a wound fell within his knowledge. Still, the few minutes until Bevor arrived were the longest of Grom's life. He rinsed the cloth and even enticed her to swallow a mouthful of water, but she didn't answer his summons.

By the time Bevor knocked, Grom was wild with worry. He growled the captain in, using the language of the wariken, incapable of forcing human speech.

To his credit, Bevor didn't ask questions. He checked the mating bite first, his brow furrowing, but he didn't offer an explanation or a plan of treatment.

"What is it?" Grom demanded, fearing the worst.

"This is no infection. The bite is healing well. Slowly, as I imagine her kind must, but well."

"What else could do this?" Was it some common illness the Wolkin carried that his mate had no immunity to?

"I cannot be sure without a full examination, but perhaps..."

"Bevor," he warned.

He winced. "The species may not be compatible."

"No. Monnan gave her to me. I will not accept that it is Her will to take Mellaia from me so soon." When the captain didn't reply, Grom bared his teeth in warning. "There must be something else. Do your examination, if you must, but find it. Whatever *it* is."

Bevor sighed, then nodded. He pulled the quilt back and reached for Mellaia. Grom grasped his wrist, narrowly squelching the urge to snap the bones for daring to touch his mate.

"Do you wish me to examine her or not?" Bevor offered calmly.

Grom released his hand, disgusted that he had to allow another male to touch his mate this way. Monnan, but he wanted to gut Bevor for presuming to look at Mellaia, but she needed his expertise. He watched every movement the captain made, jealousy nearly stealing his sanity.

Bevor touched her throat and shoulders, then her breasts. Grom tensed to attack, forcing his muscles to ease only when the captain moved on down her body. Finally, Bevor pressed at her lower abdomen. He smiled widely as she arched up with a groan.

"You're causing her pain," Grom snapped.

Bevor backed away from her. "I think not."

Grom was about to backhand the smile off the old man's face, when Mellaia moved her thighs against each other. Drops of musk gathered on her female curls. She shifted on the bed, whispering Grom's name, her nipples hard and begging for his tongue.

"Her ovum sacs are enlarged, Highness. While her species may not match ours precisely, I would wager she is at the height of her fertile cycle and seeking to carry your seed into the next generation."

Grom's cock hardened at the thought of her carrying his young. "A mating frenzy?" He hadn't expected it from another species.

"If she will tolerate it, it may be precisely what she needs to run the course of the fever."

"Will every fertile cycle pass this way?" He wasn't certain he would weather that well.

"You will have to ask your mate when she emerges. I cannot say for certain." Bevor hesitated. "Be sure she hydrates, Highness. I suspect that is the only danger to her in this."

Grom nodded, then waved Bevor away. He didn't wait for the door to close behind the captain, before he eased to the bed next to his mate.

Mellaia turned toward the movement, her lips pressing to his chest. Her hand encircled his length, searing and further arousing him at the same time.

Before Grom could order his thoughts, she'd pushed him to his back and straddled him. He stared at her, stunned by the move. In the next heartbeat, she encased him in her slick channel. She levered herself up and down his length, ripping a groan from Grom. He felt as if he was radiating the same heat she was.

He'd never considered letting Mellaia—or any female— take the lead sexually, but the sensations of her taking what she needed from him were too powerful to ignore. Though Mellaia was always responsive, the movements of her lush body against his nearly pushed him past endurance.

Grom groaned again; memories of her *magic* dance made the connection clear to him. She was using the same movements now to bring them both to climax. He thrust in counterpoint, smiling as she gasped out entreaties to Luna.

To Monnan, by the name she knows for the Goddess Dame. The Goddess brought me to her with this dance, and now She will grant us young by it. He didn't question that Mellaia would conceive; a mating frenzy would see to that.

Mellaia pressed down hard on him, her sheath milking him to climax with her. Their cries mingled. Grom had barely caught his breath and his mind was still muddled, when Mellaia started moving again.

Chapter Four

Three days later

Mellaia pushed the quilts away, uncomfortably hot beneath them. Grom touched her cheek, his hand warm against her skin, and his voice soothed her. She forced her eyes open, and he smiled.

"The fever has broken." He sounded relieved by that.

Mellaia marveled that the cuff translated their words more smoothly the longer they wore them, as if it picked up words from context and filled in the holes that were once missing in discussions.

What he said finally made it through the sleepy confusion slowing down her mind. "Fever? Was I ill?" Vague memories of Grom bathing her, feeding her, and loving her flitted through her mind. Were they memories or memories of dreams?

His smile faltered. "Is such a thing not how your mating cycle progresses?"

"Mating cycle?"

"Your fertile time?" he qualified.

Mellaia shook her head. "A woman's fertile time should pass nearly unnoticed."

Grom nodded solemnly. He whispered a prayer to Monnan—his name for Luna—for her protection and aid.

"I don't understand," she admitted.

"Neither do I. When the fever coincided with the mating frenzy and there was no sign of infection, we assumed it was normal for your people to fever at that time."

Her heart leapt in realization.

His brow furrowed, and his eyes narrowed. Grom covered her hand with his own. "Are you well?"

"I was fertile?"

Grom growled, and his cock came up again. "You were certainly receptive."

Mellaia felt her cheeks darken at her instant arousal. "Do you think I'll carry?"

He moved down her body, skating his lips over her skin. Mellaia spread for him, anticipating the rasp of his tongue between her folds, but Grom stopped at the flat span of her belly. He kissed once, then again, making her groan in awareness of him. Grom laid his cheek against the spot her womb would be largest when she carried, and she wound her fingers in his long, silken hair.

"You *will* carry," he vowed. He stroked his fingertips along the line of her hip. "I believe you might carry for me already."

Mellaia didn't question Grom's knowledge. A man who considered the magic to give them language in common a trinket must have even more impressive wonders available to him to compare it to.

She looked around at the strange room again. The walls were black as basalt, smooth as water-rolled stone, seamless, and warm to the touch. They didn't seem to be fashioned of metal, stone, or wood.

Light emanated from a portion of the wall that ran just over the top of her head. The light seemed to shine without heat indicating fire. It was steady and unwavering, and it could be ordered brighter or dimmer by her voice or Grom's alone.

The bedroom and water chamber were the only two rooms she'd seen so far, though she knew there was more outside the door. How else could Grom bring her food and drink?

"What is this place?" she asked, trusting that the cuff would make her question clear to him this time. "Is this your home?" If it was, how far had they traveled the first night? Unless it was protected by powerful magic to hide it, such a place could not be close to her village.

Grom chuckled. "No. This is not my home. It is simply the *spak*."

The cuff had also started leaving Grom's words in place when it had no idea of what word would match it in her language. "Spak?"

He raised his head, seemingly searching for a word that would translate for her. "Cart."

"Cart? But... A cart is small." This place was huge. "And...and we cannot be moving. There is no feel of the road beneath our wheels."

He smiled, his eyes twinkling in amusement. "Would you like to see?"

"Yes. I would."

Grom rose from the bed, then offered Mellaia his hand to help her up. They dressed quickly—Grom in a pair of the same soft pants and vest he wore the first night and Mellaia in a tunic that reached her knees and a cloak that dragged the ground.

He groomed her, untangling her hair and then tying it back with a length of leather. To her surprise, he didn't tie his own hair up, nor did he wear boots or offer her any sort of foot coverings.

Perhaps we are not going outside. If the structure was much larger than his rooms, who knew how far they might walk without touching open ground?

The door he used when he went for food led into a tunnel that was one of Grom's body lengths wide, five body lengths in one direction and at least ten the other. Grom led her the shorter distance, then left, into another tunnel that was just as long as the first had been. It was lined with other doors, spaced three or so body lengths apart, on either side of the tunnel.

"Cart?" she asked, certain the word had to be used in error.

He nodded.

"Ship?" she pressed. It would be a massive vessel, bigger than she'd ever dreamed possible, but it made more sense than this being a cart. Still, she no more felt the waves beneath their feet than she felt a road. The mad concept that they rode as if on wind flitted into her mind. Mellaia dismissed it promptly as wild fantasy.

Grom paused, a look of intense contemplation crinkling his features for a moment. "Ship? Yes...of a type." He pushed open a door to their left and waved her inside.

The men in the room stopped speaking at the sight of her. They stared, and Mellaia took a step backward, colliding with Grom as he moved forward. He wrapped her in his arms and growled out something that didn't translate. Nearly as a unit, the men looked away and dropped their gazes.

Grom kissed the back of her head. "All is well," he whispered.

Mellaia nodded. She went with Grom toward the center of the large room. There were wheels and levers, pieces of what looked like volcanic glass, strange writing, and multi-colored lights everywhere she looked. She ambled away from Grom, fascinated.

She reached toward a vibrant blue light, and a hand grasped at hers. Mellaia recoiled with a gasp, pulling free before the hand had a chance to clamp down on hers. In a blur of motion, Grom had the offending man by the throat, holding him just above the floor, so he had to stand on tiptoe to avoid strangling. Grom eased her behind him with a terse word of apology.

"You do not touch her," Grim stated with deadly calm. "Mellaia is my woman; not yours. Am I understood?"

The man's translated voice was muted, his actual voice rough and rasping. "Yes, my lord. I will not presume to touch your woman."

Mellaia wondered if she heard his voice in her language because Grom was near enough for his cuff to hear it or if her cuff would translate for anyone speaking his language.

A thump let Mellaia know Grom had released him. For a moment, no one moved. Mellaia hardly dared breathe.

"Come," Grom invited. "The lights are safe. Touch nothing else without asking me if it will cause harm."

She rounded his body, glancing at the man kneeling at her feet. Examining the vast array of lights seemed safer than staring at him.

Unlike the lights in the tunnels and Grom's rooms, she could see individual points of light raised from the surface of the tables and walls. Mellaia touched one after another, marveling that they created no heat.

"So beautiful," she breathed.

"It is nothing compared to your beauty."

She smiled at the compliment. "May I look out at the sea we travel?"

One man laughed harshly. Others moved away from him, and Grom glared him to silence.

Mellaia looked up at her mate. "What did I—?"

"It was inexcusably rude of him." He raised her hand and laid a kiss on the inside of her wrist. "You may indeed." Grom motioned to one of his men.

The other bowed his head, then pulled back at a lever. A section of wall slid back, and a star-filled sky appeared in the opening.

Mellaia walked to it, spellbound. Never before had she seen the stars so bright and clear. They had to be very far out to sea. *Where the waves are large, and yet I do not feel them.*

The stars were so close, she felt she could touch them...and she tried. There was a barrier blocking her, though Mellaia couldn't see it.

Disappointed, she looked down to where the sea should be. The stars continued to the edge of her field of vision. Mellaia pressed to the barrier, looking every direction. There were stars everywhere...on every side. *Stars and the darkness of deep night.*

"You sail the stars."

"Yes," Grom answered. "We do."

Her heart sounded loud in her own ears, and vertigo assaulted her. "You... You are a Son of Luna?" Was that why his man had referred to him as 'my lord'?

"We all are."

Mellaia pressed one hand to the barrier and the other to her womb. How had she been chosen for such an honor? She was a magic-woman's granddaughter, only marginally trained in the magic herself. Yet, Luna sent one of Her Prized Sons to collect Mellaia? She chose to give Mellaia to the eldest as mate? The Goddess chose her to give birth to Sons of the Night?

The concept made her dizzy.

* * * *

Her hand shook against the viewing wall, and her breathing was uneven.

Grom swallowed hard. Perhaps this had been a mistake. Her people knew nothing of star travel. Simple lights amazed them. Perhaps his bid to impress her had pushed his mate too far. "Mellaia?"

She turned toward him, her gaze averted. Without hesitation, Mellaia sank to her knees and bowed deeply to him. His men stared at her, dumbstruck by her reaction.

He ignored the breach of conduct, too concerned to give it more than passing notice. Grom gathered Mellaia into his arms, then nodded to Ter to close the panel. He strode into the corridor and toward their rooms.

When he'd closed them in together, Grom set her on her feet next to the bed. Mellaia immediately tried to sink to her knees again.

Grom pulled her up, shaking his head. "Never kneel to me."

She stammered out her agreement, though she still kept her eyes averted.

"Why do you treat me this way?" he asked, his heart aching at the change.

"Pardon, my lord. I did not know who you were."

"I am your *mate*," he growled back.

"As Luna has decreed. Oh! Mercy... You said her true name is Monnan. Am I worthy to call her — ?"

Grom captured her lips in a kiss, at a loss to reason with Mellaia any other way. She responded, and yet she was stiff in his arms.

He eased out of the kiss. "You are my mate." He would not survive her withdrawal.

"As Monnan decrees."

"No. Do not agree to give yourself to me out of fear or duty. You prayed for me, and Monnan led me to you. That much is true."

"But?" She winced, as if she felt asking it was wrong.

"Your pure response is what I crave. You've given me that until now. Do not give me less."

Mellaia raised her face, her pale blue eyes confused, seemingly pleading for guidance.

He unhooked the cloak and let it fall to the floor around her tiny feet. "Love me like you loved me before you knew who I was."

Her eyes went wide at that. He hoped she wasn't refusing.

Grom removed the tunic and tossed it to the far corner of the room. Still, she stared at him, more prey than equal. Grom shouldered off his vest, a plan taking shape.

"Dance for me," he ordered.

"Dance?"

"Call for me again. Ask Monnan who she intends to be your true mate." He circled her body, stopped to nuzzle the mating bite, and smiled at her sharply-indrawn breath. "Call me into your body as you did the first time. You do want me inside you, don't you Mellaia?"

Grom didn't give her time to answer him. He strode to the bed, stripped out of his pants, then stretched out. Mellaia was a sensual woman. This display would either spur her to dance or bring her to their bed. Either way, he would taste her fire again.

She raked a gaze up his body, her expression dazed. Just when he would was about to prompt her again, Mellaia started to move.

Her hips swiveled side to side, and his cock rose at the sight. Mellaia closed her eyes, throwing her head back as the dance became more involved.

Grom felt the wariken rising in him. She was seduction itself, capable of bringing him to his knees with a kind look. How could she fail to see it? How could such a woman ever kneel to him?

The dance held him entranced, at her mercy as she touched herself in show. As she had the first night, she cupped her breasts and offered them up for his enjoyment. Her gaze locked with his, and she moved on, down her abdomen and thighs, then between, sliding slowly up toward her core. Her scent intensified, and the dance took on a potent edge.

His muscles tensed, and he groaned. The need to bury himself inside his mate warred with the pleasure of watching her arouse herself. Her fingers worked at the front of her folds, then between, and she arched her back, soft sounds escaping her trembling lips.

"Grom." It came out a plea, and her hips jerked toward him.

That was the end of his control. He went to her, abruptly certain he knew what she wanted from him. As if confirming it for him, Mellaia gave him her back, stroking the lush curves of her ass against his weeping length.

"I am yours," he vowed. "I have been yours since the moment I saw you. Nay! Before that. The moment I scented you."

She pressed back harder, her gyrations making him mad for her.

"Do you wish me to take you as I did the first time?" *Say 'yes'. Dear Monnan, say it.*

27

"Yes. Claim me again."

Grom forced her to the floor. Mellaia laid her cheek to the rug as she had the grass in her meadow. She positioned herself for him, ass up. He thrust into her, unable to contain himself longer.

The pleading virgin of their first mating was no more. Their time together had left Mellaia a self-assured woman. She ground against him, taking what she wanted, vocalizing her pleasure with wild abandon.

He met her vigor fully, all but howling in conquest. Grom fisted his hands in the rug, burying himself to the sac with each roll of his hips.

There were no whispers of climax. It roared through her, and she screamed long and hard. Without a thought of why he would do such a thing, Grom bit into her shoulder a second time.

Mellaia moaned, her climax quickening as he thickened inside her. "So good," she gasped.

Grom bathed the new wound, praying she wouldn't react with fever again. *Unless it sparks another mating cycle. Monnan! Another three short cycles of mating frenzy would be a gift from the Goddess herself.*

"I am yours," he assured her. "You bring me to my knees."

She opened her eyes and turned her head, straining to look at him over her shoulder. Her expression told him nothing. Did Mellaia accept the power she had over him, or did she still doubt it?

"Do you understand, Mellaia?"

She nodded. A smile played at the edges of her lips.

Grom shivered as his cock released her. "What are you thinking, my mischievous mate?"

Mellaia slid off his length, moved away from him, then turned and settled between his still-fisted hands. She nuzzled Grom's face, and he tensed, hardening for her.

"You see?" he asked. "My body is at your command, answering every call."

"If that is so, perhaps I should mark you."

Grom chuckled at the suggestion. No doubt, the buck in him would resist such a thing. Still, he'd heard sexual struggles between a buck and his mate were most enjoyable. A female who challenged her mate was a rare treasure. "Perhaps you should try," he played along.

"Should I order your body then?" She was breathless, seemingly as aroused by the challenge as he was.

"Yes. I think you should." He had to convince her of her place in his life somehow.

Mellaia pushed aside at one shoulder, indicating that Grom should roll to his back. He complied, but he grasped her by the hips and drew Mellaia over him.

She rubbed her body against his, flooding his senses with stimuli of his mate. Just when he was at the edges of endurance, Mellaia shifted away. She wrapped her hand around his cock and started stroking him toward climax.

"You drive me mad," he admitted. Grom bit back a moan, as he released a bit of seed.

"I intend to."

"If you continue, my seed will be wasted." As it was, he was reining in the urge to spill to her hand.

"Never." Still, she continued.

He shifted, his nerves itching for release. "Mellaia!"

She straddled him and guided him in. "Take me," she ordered.

29

Grom didn't hesitate. He thrust into her frantically.

The first scrapes of her blunt teeth against his chest were sublime. Then she started to bite down, and instinct took over. Grom rolled Mellaia beneath him, dislodging her bite before she could break skin. He growled out his possession of her in the language of the wariken.

Mellaia wrapped herself around him, pulling him deep, inviting his control over the situation. "Come for me." It wasn't a plea. She was ordering his compliance, as he'd told her to.

His body was more than ready to comply with the order. At the first wave of his release, her fingernails bit into his back and raked hard down his flesh. Grom arched his back, forcing into her as he thickened.

Her teeth broke skin, and he closed a fist in her hair, intent on pulling her head back. Grom stilled, her climax scattering his senses. Her teeth retreated, replaced by her suckling mouth and the soft rasp of her tongue over the bite. Her tongue stroked over the nipple at the center of the bite, and Grom jerked in surprise. Mellaia started to pull away, and he flattened his hand against the back of her scalp and drew her closer.

"Don't stop," he managed. Monnan! Was this what his bite felt like for her?

When he lessened, Grom eased her head back, stunned by his actions. He'd allowed her to bite him. He'd encouraged it.

A streak of his blood marked her lower lip, and Grom stared at it, fascinated. Mellaia's eyes were half-closed, her breathing uneven. She moved sluggishly, seemingly drunken.

Yes. That is what marking her is like.

He kissed her, groaning at the taste of himself in her mouth.

Chapter Five

Nine days later

Mellaia tossed and turned, unable to sleep.

Grom turned and wrapped an arm over her. "What is it?" he grumbled sleepily.

"I'm restless. I can't... I can't settle my mind."

That seemed to wake him. "Are you ill? Are you troubled?"

"No." She sighed. "I don't know what it is."

"Are you hungry?"

"N—" Mellaia bit her lip in confusion.

"Mellaia? Are you hungry?" An edge of urgency came into his voice.

"I should not be. I ate so much." She'd eaten heartily at the last daily meal. How much could her stomach realistically hold?

"But you are." He didn't question it.

"Ravenous. Nothing satisfied. I don't know what *would* satisfy." She'd been famished, had eaten, and still she felt strangely...empty, even when her stomach had been uncomfortably full.

Grom brushed a kiss over her lips, shaking in silent laughter. "Come. The walk will help."

Grom fetched the beautiful gown of purple cloth he'd gifted her with days earlier, leaving her to see to her dressing. Then he donned his typical outfit.

He evaluated the dress, straightening the thick straps over her shoulders. They fell close to the neck, connecting at the back. It left a peephole of skin from her throat to the upper swell of her breasts. Her back was bare to lower line of her shoulder blades, displaying the healed and healing bites on her left shoulder.

As always, when they left their rooms, Grom untangled and tied back her hair. Grooming her seemed to be one of Grom's greatest delights, but he only tied her hair back when they went out among his people.

He escorted her into the tunnels, then down two levels. He opened a wide door and waved her inside. A group of women stood and bowed when they entered. Mellaia tipped her head politely. She'd learned that any further acknowledgement of their show of servitude was frowned upon.

Grom motioned to a tall, dark woman in a red dress that was cut similar to her own. "My sister, Artell."

"A pleasure," Mellaia offered.

"An honor," Artell replied. "What service may we offer?"

Grom spoke quickly, and most of the words he used didn't translate. In the end, the only things she managed to pick out were something about her hunger and food.

A smile pulled up at Artell's lips. "If you are certain, brother."

Grom darkened. "You know I'm not."

Mellaia looked from one to the other, noting Grom's unease in confusion. "Is there a problem, Grom?"

Artell offered her hand. "Not at all, Mellaia. Come. We will prepare a Wolkin delicacy. Would you like to help?"

Grom started to protest the suggestion.

His sister shot him a quelling look that actually worked. "Your mate would like to spend time in the company of other women, I am sure. You have kept her to yourself all this time."

"I would," Mellaia admitted. She slid a sideward glance at Grom, hoping he wouldn't be upset that she wanted to spend time with others, as well as him.

"You see?" Artell stated. "Women need the company of other women."

"Artell," Grom warned.

"Your mate is safe with us. If we require you, we will call for you."

Mellaia gaped at her. "Artell, is it wise — ?"

"Of course." Her smile widened. "A woman cannot thrive in the company of her mate alone."

Grom sighed. "But, why must I withdraw?"

"Some things are best imparted, woman to woman."

"They are," he conceded. "Very well " Grom kissed Mellaia solemnly. "If you need me, call for me."

She smiled. "I will."

"You see?" Artell pressed. "She glows already."

Grom scowled at her. "Immediately," he ordered, though Mellaia didn't know what he meant by it.

"Immediately," Artell replied.

He nodded and took his leave.

For a moment, no one spoke. Mellaia stared at the women nervously. She'd never been left alone with Grom's people before, but memories of the men's reactions made her wary of their feelings about Grom claiming a simple human woman as his own.

Her stomach grumbled, and Mellaia pressed the heel of her hand to it, grimacing. The pain was intense, making her head swim.

The women moved at once, guiding her to a chair. They offered her a warm tea of some sort. Artell issued orders, and they scattered. Bowls of meat and herbs appeared on the table with dizzying speed.

Mellaia sipped the tea, the ache in her stomach easing slightly.

"Better now?" Artell asked.

"Yes. Thank you, Artell."

Several of the women smiled and nodded, but they didn't address Mellaia directly. They did speak to each other while they mixed herbs, what seemed to be a discussion of family matters. Were they all related, then?

Mellaia drank the tea down, feeling relaxed to the edges of sleep, her hunger more an annoyance than a pain.

"Would you like to stir?" Artell asked.

Mellaia pulled the offered bowl toward her, lifting the spoon with a nod, taking up the task as she would have at home. Snips of conversation about children and ceremonies buzzed around her.

She paid little attention to it. The contents of the bowl had her in a state of rapture. She'd never smelled anything more appetizing in her life.

The temptation was too much for her. Mellaia pulled a cube out and popped it into her mouth, savoring the flavor. It was warm, spiced, lightly salty, moist...a delight in every way.

That taste led to another and another. She ate, feeling as if she might never be sated. If she was ever to be sated, this nectar of the Goddess alone would accomplish it.

The silence of the room registered to her abruptly. Mellaia looked up, noting the women kneeling to her in unease. What had she done to warrant this? All she'd done was eat...

What they asked me to stir.

She glanced into the bowl, dropping the spoon in shock. It was full of cubes of raw meat, coated in herbs. Her fingers were coated in the sticky blood and more stained her dress. Mellaia's mind rebelled; eating such a thing was inconceivable.

And yet, I did. Her mouth watered, demanding she continue eating it. Even now, it smelled so good, she could hardly contain herself. It tasted like sweet sap on her tongue, and she could almost swear that she felt it rushing through her veins, bringing relief to her starved body.

Mellaia pressed a hand to her mouth, stifling a sob. Surely, she was going mad.

Artell appeared at her side, pulling Mellaia into her embrace. "All is well, sister. Your young will need to eat often, and blood-rich food will be best."

"Young?" she asked.

"You carry my brother's children. Your need to sustain them is understandable."

"Is that why you knelt to me?"

"You bear for Grom, perhaps a young heir. It is an honor to be in your presence."

"I do not wish it to be this way," she pleaded. She'd hoped the women would be different.

Artell knelt next to her, wiping Mellaia's face with a cloth as soft as the dress she wore. "What do you wish?"

Mellaia met her startling green eyes. "A sister. Not servants who are honored to be in my presence but...family, as you are family to each other."

"If that is your wish, that is what we will be to you."

The others rose, rushing through simple introductions.

"Now," Artell began. "Please... Feed your young."

Mellaia stared into the bowl, torn between her mind and body. "Why meat?" she asked. "Why *raw* meat?"

Artell's smile was strained. "That is a question my brother must answer. For now, your young demand what they need. It is always wisest to listen well and follow their commands."

The scent of the offered meat had her in its thrall. Mellaia reached into the bowl again. She brought another cube to her mouth, closing her eyes in ecstasy as the warm blood teased her tongue.

* * * *

Grom paced the corridor, unable to be still until he knew for certain. The door to the kitchen opened, and he whirled toward it.

Mellaia stepped out, wrapped in the crook of Artell's arm. The smell of *aktaya* was strong, and the bodice of his mate's dress was stained in the drippings.

He howled out his triumph, then swept Mellaia into his arms. Grom laughed heartily, touching her womb. *Her bearing womb. Monnan be praised! I knew she would carry.*

Other doors opened, and curious family members peered out at them.

Grom ignored them for the moment. "Our young ate well?" he asked his sister.

Artell smiled widely. "More than my own ever did. *Aktaya,* followed by a full cup of *bluket.*"

Mellaia nestled against him, her eyes already closed, and her breathing evening out in her descent into deep sleep.

"Sleep well, sister," Artell whispered.

36

Other well-wishes followed, from the lips of the women who'd tended to her. Grom raised an eyebrow in surprise.

His sister smiled a smug little smile. "You men may stand on ceremony of chosen heir, but women are women. Your mate wishes for sisters, so sisters is what she shall have."

Grom chuckled, lifting his mate and cradling her to his chest. "Whatever my mate wants, Mellaia will have," he vowed.

"Remember that when we are delivering *aktaya* and *bluket* six times a short cycle."

"Monnan has gifted me young, Artell. They can demand the blood feast twice as often as that, and I will feed it to them personally." His heart soared at the thought of his growing young.

Artell touched Mellaia's face. "She's asleep already. Take her to bed, Grom."

He tipped his head in acknowledgement and headed back to their rooms, though he didn't doubt he would be unable to sleep for quite some time.

Mellaia settled into bed without any sign of consciousness, not that Grom had expected anything different. In the coming weeks, as their young settled into the womb, she would do little more than sleep and feast.

Chapter Six

Mellaia stretched in the bed, savoring the lingering taste in her mouth. Vague memories of the night before coalesced into the troubling truth. She opened her eyes, searching out Grom in the dim light.

He sat up in the bed beside her, watching Mellaia, a wistful expression on his face. "Are you hungry? I can bring you food."

She started to deny it, but the ache in her stomach warned it would be wise to admit it. Hadn't Artell warned that she should always do what her children demanded? "Yes. I am."

"I am not surprised. You have slept more than half a short cycle."

More than half a day. "I—I have?"

His fingertips stroked across her lips. "You have. I have longed for your waking."

Her face heated. "Why did you not wake me?"

Grom laid next to her and traced circles on her belly.

"Oh." Mellaia fought to think clearly. "Why raw meat?" she asked. "Why must our babes have raw meat?"

He sighed. "Will you eat before I answer your question?"

Mellaia laid a hand along his cheek. "I have seen your magic. You sail the stars, Grom. Monnan Herself is your *mother*. Will you hide this from me?"

He turned his head and laid a kiss in her palm. "I will not hide anything from you."

A tense moment passed, during which Grom seemed to consider how to begin. "There are many creatures that thrive in Monnan's light. Creatures that sleep the day and worship the night sky." He paused.

"Of course," she agreed. "Owls and other predators."

"Do you fear them, Mellaia?"

"Why should I? All creatures have a place in Monnan's plan. If not for the predators, animals that are sick or feeble with age would suffer on. If not for them, many would starve in the long winter."

He smiled widely. "Indeed they would. Predators are merely what Monnan made them. They are built for battle, blessed with superior sight and hearing, smell, stamina..."

Her mind worked quickly, putting the many clues into place. "Which of Monnan's Sons are you, Grom?"

"A man...when I choose to be."

"And when you do not choose to be?" Her heart skipped crazily. Hazy memories of his claiming settled in her mind. A battle had waged as he lay locked inside her body, but she'd believed it a demented dream. "A wolf," she breathed.

"An intelligent creature not unlike your wolves," he confirmed.

"May I...?" She could hardly force the words.

"You wish to see." He didn't question it.

Mellaia nodded.

Grom rose. He towered over her, his expression tortured. "Do not fear me," he pleaded. "As a man or as wariken, you are my mate. I will never harm you."

"I will not fear you." In truth, she already feared the concept that she bore children for so powerful a being. Could a frail, human woman accomplish such a thing?

The change came over him quickly. One moment, Grom leaned toward her, placing his fingertips on the edge of the bed. The next, a great wolf of nearly twice her size stood in his place. Its pelt was dark as Grom's hair, and its eyes the same golden hue as her mate's.

Mellaia paused with her hand halfway buried in his pelt, nearly groaning at how soft it was. She sought out the beast's gaze, seeking permission to continue. The eyes were intelligent, warm...inviting.

"Grom."

He licked her cheek, prompting a giggle from her in response. Mellaia stroked his fur, murmuring her perceptions aloud. As if showing how pleased he was with her response, Grom settled his great head in her lap.

Peace descended on her troubled mind. Grom would not permit her to be harmed in giving life to his children. He would never allow any harm to come to her.

Chapter Seven

Two and a half weeks later

Grom took the empty bowl from Mellaia's hand, smiling as she sucked the blood and calming herbs from her fingertips. She drank down the cup of warmed, spiced blood as if she were still starved.

"Should I send for more?" he offered.

Mellaia blushed deeply and didn't reply, though she licked the slick of blood from her lips.

He sighed. How many times would he have to repeat it?

"I know," she interrupted the first word of his speech. "The babes will ask for what they need, and denying them will be very uncomfortable." She rubbed at her lower back.

Grom took over, massaging at her tense muscles. "And I become legendary," he teased. Already, the needs of his young had raised more than a few eyebrows in shock. Some short cycles, she required the blood feast eight times. Such need was unheard of.

"You do?"

"The crew are taking bets on how many you carry and how big they will be at birth."

"They are not," she protested.

"They are."

"Why?"

Because it's likely you carry the next heir to the throne. But there was more. "Even Artell and I didn't eat this much. Your womb already protrudes."

She scowled at the reminder.

"And I love it," he hastened to add.

"If you say that again, I will order you to prove you love it and feast on your blood." Though her words were harsh, she nipped at his shoulder.

"My blood is strong." Monnan! Feeding their young on his own body was an erotic delight he'd never dreamed of. Usually only women were so blessed.

"And your cock?" she taunted.

He pushed her back into the cushions at the head of the bed, then dragged the warm gown Artell had given her up to Mellaia's hips. She raised her core for him, and Grom thrust deep.

"Stronger," he gasped.

But his self-control was weak. Luckily, hers was as weak as his. It ended quickly, her climax spurring his, her bite playing sweet counterpoint to the soft grip of her sheath on his increased girth.

For several minutes, they lay locked together, his hands buried in her hair, his blood flowing over her massaging tongue. Then his cock lessened, and she sank to the bed, a soft sigh announcing her relaxation.

"Should I send for more food?"

Mellaia shook her head. "No. But I am thirsty."

"Water or *bluket*?"

Her nose scrunched up as if in distaste.

"Mellaia, what do you require?"

"Milk."

He stared at her, shocked nearly beyond words. "Already?"

Most females ate nothing but *aktaya* and *bluket* for a full moon cycle after the cravings settled. Milk and marrow supplemented from that point until the fifth moon cycle, and all manner of cravings struck after that. Mellaia had only enjoyed the blood feast for two short cycles less than three large phases of the moon, more than a phase less than the usual moon cycle. Hardly enough time to abandon endless slumber.

"Are you certain?" he asked. "If you drink milk too soon, it will cause your stomach to cramp and empty."

Her resolute glare and the arms crossing over the slight swell of his young left no room for argument.

Grom rose and dressed for the trip to the kitchen. She pulled herself up from the bed, clearly intent on accompanying him. He walked beside her, unspeaking, troubled. He had to trust her instincts, though she wasn't Wolkin. Still, if he trusted her and she was wrong, he would blame himself for it.

Damn! Having a mate of another species is nerve-wracking.

At the kitchen, he settled her in a chair and went to the cooling unit that contained milk and egg products. He filled a mug with milk, then turned to her. Forcing his arm to extend taxed his instincts.

"Grom, no!" Artell came from the far door, her hand out to snatch the mug from him.

The stress snapped him. Grom wrenched away from his sister, growling out a warning at her invasion of his space. Her mate, Broll, bolted into the room. He dragged Artell behind his body, his growl deepening as Grom's did.

"No," Mellaia shouted. She came to her feet and slammed her hands down on the metal counter.

Artell made soothing sounds, trying to talk Broll down. Mellaia stepped up behind Grom, doing the same for him. Sanity came slowly to each buck.

"Please, no," Mellaia whispered. "He only means to protect his mate. You know he does."

"So do I!" But her hands and voice turned wariken into pup. Grom settled into a chair, then buried his face in the mound of their young. The scent of their loving comforted him.

Mellaia stroked her hands through his hair. She sang softly in her own language. Grom ignored the translator cuff. The words weren't important; the soothing emotions were the key.

His hand was abruptly empty.

"No," Artell ordered again.

Grom tensed, and Mellaia shushed him. His mate's voice was sharper than his wariken teeth.

"If one more of you tells me that the babes will demand what they need, but then denies me what they clearly demand, I may sprout teeth to match my mate's."

Artell stammered out the reasons Mellaia shouldn't try to drink milk yet.

"Enough," Grom barked. He stood, feeling weary. "The young do not speak to me. They speak to Mellaia. Though it makes me crazed to let her risk the rejection, it makes me more crazed to make her risk the pain of denying our young."

"Oh, Grom." Artell sighed, then waved Mellaia on.

He met Mellaia's eyes, content that there would be no more interruptions or protests. "Drink it. If our young demand this, by Monnan, drink it."

She hesitated only a moment, then drank the mug of milk down in a series of deep swallows. Grom placed his hands on her shoulders, waiting for any sign of distress. He pushed away the thought that he would wear her meal, if she rejected it. If she brought it back, it would be what he deserved for allowing her to endanger herself.

Broll prayed aloud to Monnan, no doubt anticipating Grom's fury when his mate fell ill.

"Mellaia?" he prompted her.

She smiled widely. "Good." She laughed a tinkling little laugh that made her sound drugged.

"Good?" he asked cautiously.

"Magical. Wonderful. Can I have more?"

"Artell!"

His sister rushed to take the mug, then sprinted to the cooling unit.

Broll gasped out a prayer of thanks. He sank to one knee and bowed his head deeply. "Truly, Grom is hand chosen for his place. As is his mate."

Artell brought the milk back to Mellaia, and his mate drank the second mug as quickly as the first. At last, she let out a sigh and sank to Grom's chest.

"Should I add milk to the trays?" Artell asked.

Grom chuckled. "And marrow. Only a young heir could demand so much of his dame."

"Or her dame," Artell reminded him.

He shot his sister a smile. "There hasn't been a female chosen first in centuries. If any woman could bear it, Mellaia can."

His mate broke into their banter by requesting another mug of milk.

Chapter Eight

Two months later

"We have really come around?" Mellaia asked, her mind reeling at the fact that she'd no more felt that than she'd felt their passage through the depths of space for the last four months.

"Yes, Lady Mellaia," Broll replied crisply.

He spoke to her, but he didn't meet her eyes. To this day, Mellaia wasn't certain whether Broll felt he was beneath her or he feared Grom's jealousy.

She smoothed the dress Artell and the other women had fashioned for her introduction into Wolkin society. It was the same purple as the other dresses she'd worn, and it still bared her back and shoulders to the upper swell of her breasts, but this one had no straps, had long sleeves that covered her from a hand-width beneath the shoulder to mid-hand. It was also cut to accommodate her rapidly-growing children.

Though she was little more than halfway through a Wolkin seven-month pregnancy, she was nearly the size of a full-term human pregnancy. Mellaia worried about that most of all. Human women were not made to grow so big.

Grom appeared at her side, massaging her back and womb. He scowled and touched the tight little braids the women had pulled her hair into. "Was that necessary?" he demanded.

She reached back to smooth the braids, conscious of mussing them. "Artell said it was traditional. Is it not?"

For his answer, he quickly unbound the braids near the front of her head, creating a cascade of waves that surrounded her face and flowed nearly to her hips. "The back may stay as it is."

"To show your mark, of course," she teased.

His smile made her made her heart skip beats. "Would you deny me my right to announce that you are mine?"

"I am proud to be yours."

Grom raised an eyebrow in challenge. "Just proud?"

She laughed heartily, then drew his hand to their babes. "You know there is more."

He nodded, seemingly relieved. "Good."

A wickedly appealing thought settled in her mind. Mellaia pulled his vest aside to uncover the faint proof of her marks on Grom. "Perhaps I should announce you are mine as well."

In truth, there wasn't much to show. Grom's people healed faster and more completely than humans did. A broken pink oval was all the sign there was of the half-dozen times she'd bitten him.

His expression intense, he stripped off the vest, folded it, and tucked it into the waist of his purple trousers. "I want you to. I want no one to doubt you are my equal, my match, in every way."

At a loss for words, Mellaia drew his mouth down to hers. Grom didn't question her intent. The kiss was hot, intense, a clear indication that only the presence of his people stood between them and the usual conclusion to such a kiss.

He pulled away at a strange sound not unlike wind through the treetops. "It is time."

Mellaia nodded, forcing a smile to her face though her nerves were on edge.

She'd learned many things in the months they'd traveled the stars. Grom hadn't been directly born of Monnan's loins, but rather, he was a direct descendant of one of Her Prized Sons. Her mate was blessed, royal, but not a god himself. That discussion had taken place when Mellaia had gone into hysterics at the idea of meeting Grom's mother.

To her surprise, the doors opened to reveal a clear night sky. Mellaia pondered that. Had their sleep cycle always fallen in the day? Grom's people were Monnan's children. It was likely she'd lived a night-hunter's life with him.

Grom took her hand, allowing Captain Bevor and his mate to lead the way down the long ramp. Artell and Broll followed closely after, their two young boys holding to their parents' inner hands, probably to keep them away from the edge of the ramp. When his sister touched soil, Grom started escorting Mellaia down the ramp.

A murmur of whispering rose, mixing with night sounds. The assembled Wolkin stared, and Mellaia forced herself not to slide closer to Grom. She was mate to their heir, their prince, his equal in every way; she would not show fear.

A man at the far end of the path stood abruptly, and Mellaia faltered. Grom squeezed her hand in comfort and led her onward. Artell's two boys broke from their parents and raced past Bevor to leap into the older man's arms. After a moment, he set them on the chair he'd vacated.

The man resembled Grom, save the white patches in his dark hair. He wore purple trousers as his son did, topped with a gold vest with purple trim. A woman stood and came to his side. She wore a dress not unlike the one Mellaia was wearing with a golden cloak.

The rest of the Wolkin became little more than a blur of color: a wide array of tan, brown, and black hair...of green, gold, or brown eyes. They wore bright colors not of the royal purple, gold, and red.

The captain and his mate knelt to the leaders, then faded into the crowd. Artell and Broll knelt, then moved to the queen's side. That left no one to shield Mellaia from their gazes.

The queen smiled, then spoke softly to her mate. He nodded in response, though his eyes were hard and cold.

Still, Mellaia kept her chin up and her back straight. To her amazement, the queen's smile put her at ease. Her heart rate slowed, and her grip on Grom's hand loosened.

They stopped little more than an arm's length away from his parents, and Mellaia tipped her head in a sign of respect. She pulled the greeting Grom taught her from her memory.

"Hon mar ta dame a mar maarr, Grom."

No one moved for two dozen heartbeats, and Mellaia slid a questioning look at her mate, afraid she'd pronounced it wrong, despite weeks of practice. The rumbling sound for the word 'mate' in the ancient form of their language was so foreign to her, it had defeated her many nights before she'd perfected it.

Did I? Monnan, tell me I haven't offended them.

"My son has brought us quite the surprise," the queen noted. "Does your mate not deserve a proper introduction to us, Grom?"

"Does she not deserve a proper welcome from my sire?" he countered.

"She does, indeed."

The king looked as if he might refuse, then he stepped forward and laid his cheek alongside Mellaia's. He took a deep breath, then cupped his large hand over the mound of her babes. They moved against him as if in recognition.

His hand jerked slightly, and he gasped. "Dear Monnan! You are most welcome, daughter."

Mellaia didn't doubt he was sincere. "My thanks. It would be an honor to call you 'sire'."

He stepped back and cupped both hands around her womb. The babes kicked furiously.

"They are very strong young."

Mellaia bit back a wince, then forced a chuckle. "Like their sire."

"Like their dame," Grom added. "My sire, Derr, and my dame, Zella."

"Most honored," Mellaia greeted them.

"I present my mate, Mellaia."

Zella stepped forward, and Derr cleared the way for his mate. She repeated the motions Derr made. Again, the babes leapt at the connection.

She stepped back, surveying Mellaia's womb with a critical eye. "Do you eat marrow?" she inquired.

"Yes. I do."

Artell laughed heartily. "A full half moon cycle earlier than any dame I have ever encountered and milk nine short cycles earlier than that. These young eat like crawling nursers and have since their first scent of *aktaya* and *bluket*."

Mellaia's cheeks burned in embarrassment at such avid attention to her bodily needs. *These are their grandchildren. They are likely concerned.*

"What are the wagers?" Derr asked.

Grom responded eagerly to that, making Mellaia wonder how closely he followed the games. "Heavily on three young at five bluestone and nine cycles early. Again, but lesser, at four young at four bluestone and ten cycles early."

"Three at seven and twelve cycles," Derr predicted.

Zella stroked Mellaia's womb again. "Two young at ten and twelve cycles," she stated firmly.

"Ten?" her mate scoffed. "No young weighs more than seven. There must be more than two."

"More young would mean eating more of the same. I stand by my prediction that the composition is the tell of larger young."

"As you wish. Five opal on each."

Zella smiled. "Are you ready to feast, Mellaia?"

"Endlessly," she admitted.

"Change mine to two young at ten and thirteen cycles."

Grom chuckled. "As you wish, Dame Zella."

* * * *

"Artell tells me you are a priestess of Monnan?" Zella inquired.

All around the table, heads turned, and voices dropped off.

Mellaia swallowed the mouthful of milk. "Yes. I am not a mistress priestess yet. I suppose I never shall be now. I was training with my grandmother. She is the mistress of our village."

There was a moment of stillness. Zella offered her hand. "Come. I wish to show you something."

She hurried to join Grom's dame, and the two males followed along. Zella went to two large doors on one side of the massive hall, and Derr pushed them open for her.

Mellaia gasped at the sight of the chamber beyond. "A moon temple." She'd only been permitted to enter their own moon temple for the last year.

"Yes, it is." Zella waved her on.

Mellaia wandered in, looking up at the open roof. "Does it have a shield?" *It must. Otherwise, the temple would be weather-worn.*

"Most astute," Derr replied. "It does."

"We didn't have your magic. We had to lay covers in foul weather to avoid damage." She went to the altar, and stared at it in confusion. Without considering her actions, Mellaia reached out to move the elements into the proper positions. She stopped a fingertip away from the first, and looked to Grom.

He nodded. "We have not had a trained priestess in generations."

You still do not. Not fully trained.

Derr took over for him. "It would be an honor to have the magic of Monnan's worship returned to Wolkin."

Grumbling from the main room said not everyone agreed with his decision.

Mellaia arranged the elements in their intended places. "These offerings are old?"

Zella appeared at her side. "They are. Ancient."

"They should be replaced with new at the start of every new year."

Derr barked something that didn't translate, and there was a rush of feet away and then back again. Two young women stopped on the opposite side of the altar from her, carrying the necessary elements.

Mellaia took a calming breath. "Build a fire in the pit." She nodded toward the proper place. "The old elements must be burned, and the new put in their place. Monnan will surely forgive the poor timing, due to the circumstances."

No one moved for a moment. Then Derr started giving commands.

* * * *

Grom watched his mate work, spellbound by the graceful movements of her hands. She carefully emptied each small pot into a bowl, brushed away the dust of the old, and set it aside. Once all six pots were emptied, she ordered her female attendants to dump the leavings into the roaring fire and to stoke it high. She started filling the pots again, whispering prayers to Monnan as she did it.

With each back in its place, she looked up. "I need a bit of kindling wood to carry flame from the pit to the altar."

One of the servants rushed to comply. After Derr's first warning, they had been quick to follow any orders Mellaia gave. Those watching at the doorway parted to allow the young female to pass back and forth with the requested wood.

Mellaia took it with a word of thanks. She walked to the raging fire, and Grom intercepted her, holding her hand just outside the range of the flames.

His mate shot him a warning look. "I have been feeding and seeding fires since I was little more than toddling, and the priestess lights the sacred flame." She pulled at his hold. "If you would..."

He released her with a tip of his head, reining in his instincts to shield her from any possible harm that might befall her.

In moments, she'd lit the bit of wood. She glided back to the altar, and Grom's muscles eased with each step she took away from the larger fire. The fire she lit on the altar was warm and inviting. He could understand why their ancestors had embraced these rituals. A sense of calm descended on the chamber.

She lifted the dagger from the altar and brought the blade to her fingertip. Realization of what she intended made his heart stutter.

"Wait!"

Mellaia sighed. "It is only a bit of blood, Grom. If I do not complete the ritual, I offer offense to the goddess Monnan."

He strode to the opposite side of the altar from her position and thrust his arm across it. "Take mine. I offer it willingly, for Monnan and for you."

She seemed to struggle for words for a moment, and her pale eyes widened. "You cannot."

"Why?"

"It must be the priestess officiating. I have done so before," she hastened to add. "Really. It will not harm me."

You have not done so while I watched. His teeth itched in the need to rip something apart. At last, he drew his arm back and waved her on.

Mellaia hesitated only a moment. Then she sliced a small cut in the tip of her pointing finger and pressed it to the etched design on the edge of the altartop. Her voice rose in a song to Monnan. At the crescendo, she plunged the dagger into a notch at the center. of the altar.

Soft blue-purple light erupted upward, passing through the moon-view at the top of the temple. Mellaia backed away with a gasp. Her gaze trailed upward, following the light...just in time for it to disappear.

"What was that?" Zella asked, clearly as awe-struck as Grom was himself.

"I don't know," Mellaia replied. "I have never encountered such an outward sign of the Goddess's magic before." She took a step forward and stroked the edge of the altar with her uninjured hand. The light burst to life again.

Sounds of appreciation went up from those gathered outside the temple.

Mellaia pulled her hand back and looked at it, and the light disappeared again.

"It responds to touch, now that it is activated," Derr opined. He reached out and touched the altar. Nothing happened. After a moment, he eased his hand back. He stared at Zella, clearly at a loss to explain it. A look of realization lit his face. "Females. Perhaps it only responds to females. Try it." He waved his mate on.

She touched the edge, but nothing happened. Then Zella waved the young females toward the altar. They looked as if the idea of touching it frightened them, but each tried. Nothing happened.

When the last one backed away, Grom smiled. "Touch it, Mellaia."

She hesitated, then grasped the design with her still-bleeding hand. Again, the light roared to life. After a moment, she removed the dagger from the notch. Still, the light rose in the beacon toward the night skies. Mellaia released the altar and settled the dagger at the base of the design of offerings with a deep bow. The light faded away, and Grom let out a breath he hadn't realized he'd been holding.

He circled the altar to her side. He took the dagger and raised her uninjured hand, then settled the weapon in her palm.

"I shouldn't," Mellaia managed weakly. "I am not a fully-trained mistress priestess yet. I am not worthy to—"

"I believe Monnan has just stated otherwise."

She nodded solemnly, and her gaze traveled toward the moon-view. "I believe you may be correct."

Zella wrapped an hand around Mellaia's arm. "You must tell us what you need to act as a proper priestess to Monnan. Whatever you need will be provided for you." Grom had never seen his dame so excited before, even following the birth of Artell's young.

"I should train another priestess. There should always be two." Mellaia held herself rigidly still, as if waiting for some protest to her training one of Grom's people in their shared religion.

As if someone would dare!

To his shock there was a snort of derision from the crowd. The entire royal family turned to glare at the male who'd loosed it. Grom's temper spiked at the sight of Kobie, the same cousin who'd dared try to touch Mellaia aboard ship.

"You have a problem, Kobie?" he challenged.

His cousin took his time, swallowing down a mouthful of blood wine. He shrugged. "We shall see."

"See what?" Derr interrupted. "What is your basis for this rude reaction to your new princess?"

Though Grom's blood burned to defend his mate, he deferred to his sire in counseling their people. *For the moment.*

Kobie scowled. "We shall see, in time, whether this off-worlder can produce strong young ones worthy of the throne."

"Yes, we shall," Derr growled him down.

The beta male bowed slightly and retreated.

Mellaia shifted in discomfort, her face flaming, and her expression imperfectly masked from him. She was upset. She was embarrassed.

And I must let my sire handle the situation. Damn this!

He raised her bleeding hand and sucked the injured fingertip into his mouth. As always, her blood went to his head and engaged his senses.

Mellaia snapped her gaze to his face, and her body prepared for him.

Before he could suggest it, his dame beat him to the words. "Take her to bed, Grom. We can learn what else Mellaia needs for the temple at first meal."

He smiled at his parents and wished them good sleep. Then he led Mellaia through the parting crowd and took her to his rooms. *Our rooms now.*

His mate sank against his chest and wrapped her arms around him. Though she was aroused, she was also troubled.

"Mellaia?" he prompted her.

"He's dangerous, Grom."

It took him only a heartbeat to catch up with her logic trail. "Kobie?"

She nodded.

"I will not allow Kobie to harm you, and neither will anyone in my immediate family." It was a vow he was confident of.

"I know, but he's dangerous. I feel it. He intends something. Maybe not this short cycle or this moon cycle, but he has a plan, and whatever it is, it isn't good for us."

A shiver worked down Grom's spine. He'd only heard a prophecy once in his life, but he recognized the tone. The fur at the base of his skull rose in warning, and he determined to let Derr know about the threat at his first possible opportunity.

For now, his only aim was to put his mate at ease in her new home.

Chapter Nine

"You're certain?" his sire asked again.

"It was a prophecy. I have no doubt. Mellaia had channeled Monnan's power. She'd been touched by the Goddess Herself. Her words could have been nothing else."

Derr seemed to consider that carefully. "I believe you."

He didn't need to say more. "Others will not."

"No. There are...expectations. Even as Lord of the Land, I cannot simply execute another without proof of their treachery."

It was true, though Grom cursed it. "We must wait for him to act. I suppose it is well enough, for now, that we *know* the attack is coming, whatever it is."

Derr grumbled his agreement, sounding more like a tree-climber than a wariken. "I will see to it. Guard her well, Grom."

He scowled at his sire, offended that Derr thought such a thing needed to be vocalized. A smile softened the old man's face, letting Grom know he'd been joking.

This is no joking matter.

His sire strolled away before Grom could find his voice...or his claws.

Smart move.

He followed the sound of Mellaia's voice to the table and smiled widely at the sight of her.

Mellaia ate *aktaya* with her left hand, using her right to sketch something on the art board set between herself and Dame Zella. Servants rushed back and forth, setting out *bluket* and milk, sneaking peeks at whatever she was working on.

"I see," Dame Zella said. "The ceremonial gown is, in essence, two gowns, one worn over the other."

"Yes."

Grom bit back a grimace. It sounded like far too many clothes for his mate to be wearing.

Then again... Officiating before countless males? Best that she wear as many clothes as possible to dissuade them. After all, what male wouldn't be attracted to Mellaia?

His dame spoke again. "You said you have need of females to assist you and to be your second."

Mellaia nodded, swallowing a masticated cube of *aktaya*. "The assisting females should be a mixed group of ages, from before adolescence to adult...but none who have carried babes or carry now."

"Easily done," Dame Zella replied. "Would you like to choose them?"

"Since I do not know them yet, I would ask you to. They should be responsible females...but not too meek."

She smiled. "Monnan respects a strong female."

"True. My second must be at least my age and must have borne young already. Since she must be expected to take over all the duties of the mistress, should anything befall me—"

Grom tensed at the thought of such a horror.

"—she must be a dame or crone. A dame would be better, to give us ample time to train the third after her, Monnan willing."

That intrigued Grom. "Were you second in your village?" *She couldn't have been. Could she?*

Mellaia's cheeks darkened, and she cleared her throat. "Third. A female may be trained before she bears, but she may not become a mistress until she has. *Grandmother* had a second mistress who was a dozen years my elder."

He took a seat at the table across from them, his interest piqued. Connections made him uneasy, but he had to ask the question. "Was that why you were calling a mate to you with your magic dance?"

She didn't shy from his gaze. On one hand, that made him proud. On the other, it told him he might not care for her answer.

"It was. I had found no male in my village appealing, and I could not advance in my studies until I had a mate. Appealing to the Goddess seemed the best route to finding one." Her lips curved in a sweet, little smile. "You must admit, She heard and answered my prayer."

Grom couldn't help but return her smile. He'd known from the beginning that she'd had her reasons for calling for a male. He'd stupidly assumed they were all sexual reasons, but since the sexual side of their union was—in no way—lacking, why complain?

"I see," Kobie drawled from the far corner of the room.

Was he spying on Mellaia? It seemed likely. *What is your game, cousin?*

Kobie continued before Grom could decide whether or not to question him.

"That means you lack full knowledge of Monnan's ways."

Mellaia stiffened at the accusation. "That would be incorrect. A training priestess has access to all the sacred texts and assists in all manner of rituals. The only thing she cannot do until she is a dame is officiate. I have proven capable of it."

"I see."

Grom glared at him, his loathing of that phrase growing with each repetition of it. Again, Kobie forged on before he could question his meaning.

"If you require a dame as your second, perhaps you would consider my mate, Duella. She bears at the moment, as you do yourself."

His tone was sweetly ingratiating.

He hopes to gain something from this. Perhaps the status of having a priestess wife.

Mellaia didn't answer promptly; instead, she seemed to weigh her options. Grom cursed his inability to counsel her, in this case. Any instruction on Wolkin laws and mores he gave her would be perceived as a move against Kobie.

Still... *Please do not accept. Even if you defer on a decision, it gives us time to reject Duella in a non-confrontational way that Kobie cannot use against us.*

She took a deep breath, then met Kobie's gaze directly. "Possibly as a third, when we are ready to take one on. The training will be stressful. I believe a woman who is not currently bearing would be best."

Grom smiled. "Understood. We can compile a list of—" Her tension stopped him cold.

Mellaia hurried into an answer to his unasked question. "I have already asked Artell to train as my second. She is prepared to do so. Excited to."

"Without giving consideration to all possible candidates?" Kobie challenged her choice.

"Artell was already interested in what I knew of Monnan's ways. We've had many discussions about it aboard ship. Since she was interested in the position, it only made sense to choose someone who had already learned so much."

Kobie opened his mouth—most likely to protest—and Zella cut him off.

"Duella had her opportunity to make herself known to Mellaia aboard ship, as the other women have. Do not think her snub has gone unnoticed."

Grom stiffed at that pronouncement. He hadn't known his mate had been snubbed, would have taken a very dim view of it had he known it. *Why didn't Artell tell me?*

Mellaia stared at him, her back straight, her expression neutral and cool. Only the slight movements of her hands in her lap announced her nervous state in the face of Kobie's anger.

"She was *bearing.* I pampered her, as a solicitous mate should."

Mellaia spoke up abruptly, ice in her tone. "A woman cannot thrive in the company of her mate alone. A woman must have the company of other women. Perhaps you should not have isolated her so completely."

He gaped at her, but Grom noticed Kobie didn't deny he'd been the one to keep Duella from Mellaia.

How did she know it? Perhaps it is something women speak of between themselves.

"Artell *will* be trained as my second."

A true royal mate. If Mellaia feared she'd overstepped her boundaries, she gave no sign of it to their adversary.

Grom smiled at her. "Good. Training can begin at once."

From the corner of his eye, Grom saw Kobie darken, his jaw tighten in fury. He gave the other male his full attention. "Was there anything else?" Grom asked, falsely calm when he boiled inside.

"Not at all." Kobie turned away. "I simply have other matters to attend to."

"I see," Grom offered his usual reply.

Kobie bristled visibly, hesitated, then started moving away without comment.

In the stillness following his exit, Zella sighed. "I have never trusted that wariken."

Grom agreed completely with the observation.

* * * *

Mellaia nodded, her mouth full of milk. Beside her, Grom roared in laughter. His sire joined in.

Zella gaped at her. "Your dame allowed you to engage in such antics? Dear Monnan, you could have been killed." She paled a notch, probably at the thought of it.

She sobered a bit. "My dame died when I was a toddling babe. A fever took her and my sire within half a moon. My *grandmother* raised me, but as priestess, she had many duties that kept her attention focused elsewhere. I often wandered off to my own amusements." Mellaia raised her cup for another drink.

Whatever protest Zella was about to make was drowned out by Kobie's snide tone.

"Criminals and cowards are often fleet of foot."

She choked on the mouthful of milk in surprise, then forced it down painfully.

Grom was already on his feet, dark fur sprouting and receding in waves down the length of his arms.

"And those bred from criminals and cowards," he continued.

Derr waved Grom back, then focused on Kobie. "Explain yourself before I have you punished as a traitor to your princess."

Kobie's eyes went wide in what she was sure was fake shock. "I meant no disrespect to Mellaia, of course. I was simply musing on the subject of her ancestry."

Her hands shaking, Mellaia gripped the cup hard. "My people are *not* criminals and cowards. They fought bravely against Grom's men. Or perhaps you were not there for the battle? Were you hiding in the ship?" She was sure she hadn't seen all the men with Grom that night, but her instincts told her Kobie had not been among them. She drew in a deep breath; though it was ridiculous to believe she could take in his scent as Grom's people did, the move only reinforced her certainty.

Kobie's eyes narrowed, and the back of her neck itched. Ignoring it and acting unaffected taxed her patience.

Surely the itching is a bad omen.

Grom snorted, and she saw a flash of his fangs.

"He was on *duty*," Grom confirmed.

"That was the schedule." Kobie shrugged as if it was of no importance.

"Then how can you claim knowledge of Mellaia's people?" Derr inquired coolly.

Kobie shifted in his seat, taking his time forming an answer. "It occurred to me that it was wild chance to encounter a race that so closely resembled us that they are capable of unassisted reproduction with our kind. I was...intrigued, so I searched the library of exploration. I found that we had visited that world several times before." He took a deep drink of his blood wine.

The entire room seemed to hold a collective breath.

Just as he intends. He is the center of attention for all.

"We lost a crewmember there. A battle surgeon. He stole weaponry, books, and medical supplies, then disappeared into the mountains with some of the primitives who inhabited the world."

Grom fairly vibrated in fury. "And your point is...?"

"Only that your mate's people would no-doubt be the offspring of that male, most likely initially created by way of our own science, with stolen information from the ship."

Zella and Derr shared a look Mellaia couldn't fathom.

Derr took the lead. "What are you saying? That you believe Mellaia is somehow tarnished by what *may* be an ancestor's failing?"

"I wouldn't say tarnished, precisely," he offered diplomatically.

"That's good," Zella offered drily, "for *you*, Kobie."

His brow creased, and he stiffed slightly.

It wasn't the response he expected to hear.

"Pardon, Dame Zella?"

She stirred her blood wine with one long claw.

A warning for him. Mellaia didn't question it.

"It occurred to *me* that we knew little about the man who'd married our dear cousin Duella. To that end, I embarked on research of my own."

His features darkened, but Kobie didn't reply.

"While we *may* have visited Mellaia's world four or six hand of generations ago, one of your ancestors *did* self-injure to avoid battle less than a tenth of that time ago. Were we to make such assumptions, your blood has been less diluted than Mellaia's."

It was clear Kobie wanted to voice a protest, but he remained wisely silent.

Zella sighed, then rose from her place at Derr's side, leaving her blood wine behind. She made a show of giving Kobie her back. "Mellaia, would you be so kind as to mix me one of your sleep teas?"

"Of course." Mellaia hurried to comply, the back of her neck still itching and burning in warning.

* * * *

"And this," Derr announced, opening the box the held the testing stone.

"The heart stone," Mellaia finished excitedly. "I was not certain you had one."

Grom stared at her, startled by the comment. *I so often am when Mellaia proves her knowledge of Monnan's ways. I underestimate her far too often.* It was a failing he should try harder to rise above, he decided.

Artell nodded. "Yes. It is. Did you test well with the stone?"

It was a common question, but Mellaia seemed confused by it.

"Test? The heart stone consecrates."

For a moment, no one spoke.

Mellaia fidgeted a bit. "It introduces babes to Monnan's light," she insisted.

Artell sighed. "It does. It also tests for leadership ability."

She sank to the bench, seemingly lost in thought. "Oh. I...suppose we have used it thus, though we never thought of it that way. And we believed it showed strength of will and of heart."

Grom sat to one side of her, and Artell took the other, leaving Derr standing over them.

"So you know the proper ceremony then?" Derr asked.

"It is the first we learn. Any priestess and even trainees can officiate."

"One of the reasons we still know how to use the stone," he grumbled in reply.

"Those who pulsed with power became your leaders?" Grom asked, directing Mellaia's attention away from the reason they didn't have priestesses at the time of her arrival.

Mellaia shook her head. "We lead by *council*."

Grom looked around, hoping someone understood the alien term. *No sign of it. I loathe when the translator fails.*

She sighed, clearly coming to the same conclusion he had. "A group of elders make decisions for the village, as a whole. The mistress is always one of the elders called to serve on the *council*. *Lument* are as well. The other spots are taken by those who are known for their wisdom and courage."

He decided to ignore the second alien word for a moment, and smiled though he found the concept odd. "What do those who pulse with power do in your society?" She'd said it held meaning for her. Perhaps the word she'd used would be explained by asking.

"Females become priestesses, mistresses in their time. Strong light that does not pulse in a female's...testing means she may become a second, should it please her to do so."

"You pulsed in power?" Derr asked, fairly wiggling in excitement as a child might.

Mellaia cocked her head to one side as if his sire's question confused her. "Of course. Did I not just say as much?"

Grom straightened in pride. *We were both chosen in test. Our young will be strong. The strongest our people have seen in generations.*

"What about males who pulse in power?" Artell asked.

"The *Lument*?"

Ah, that is what the word means.

"If that is what your people call them," Artell confirmed.

Mellaia smiled widely. "They undergo a quest into the mountains...alone. If they return alive with the skin of a great beast, they can present it to any unmated woman in the village and claim her as his own. It is an ancient tradition."

Grom scowled. "Do you wish the hide of a great beast, Mellaia? If you do, I will provide one, according to your customs." If she felt cheated by the lack of tradition, he would bend. A woman like her was worth any danger.

She laughed heartily, then laid a hand on his arm, offering him a pleased little smile. "No. Even if Kobie is correct about my people's origins, you are not one of them. My sire captured my dame with a *bear's* skin. We captured each other with Monnan's magic."

His blood heated at the memory, and his cock rose in response.

A blush darkened her cheeks. "Should I dance for you again tonight?" she offered.

Grom growled, his wariken barely in check. Everyone else, save Mellaia, wisely decided to abandon the room to them.

Chapter Ten

Mellaia finished the song of introduction, listening to Artell's echo with a smile for the new dame. Artell had told her the full rite had not been used since the loss of their priestesses. For generations, they'd had nothing but the most cursory introduction to Monnan's light.

How incredibly sad.

Duella cradled one babe in each arm, happier than Mellaia had ever seen her. The bed she was laying on had fine, soft linens and thick cushions. Lacking though Kobie might be in other ways, he had provided well for his mate.

And Kobie is honored to have his babes the first given a full introduction, as all children deserve.

"Name your young," Mellaia requested.

"My daughter...my firstborn is Elyss. My son, Evio."

By the flash of fang in Kobie's scowl, Mellaia guessed he didn't like the names she'd chosen.

So sad for you, Kobie. Naming is a dame's right, in both our cultures.

She focused on Duella, ignoring the unpleasant sire. "Elyss, so named, know the touch of our goddess, Monnan."

Mellaia placed the heart stone on the babe's chest, and it glowed brightly. *Not the next mistress, but perhaps a lower priestess.*

Duella laughed in delight. "I knew it. I knew she would test well."

She tipped her head in response, then collected the heart stone and reached for the younger babe. "Evio, so named, know the touch of our goddess, Monnan."

The stone glowed, but weakly.

Mellaia bit back a wince. She forced a smile for the stricken dame. "A fine son. He will have your sweet nature, Duella."

I've never had to make apologies before. Among my people, one either pulsed or did not. Pulsing or strong light meant a calling. A faint reading may mean something as simple as a not-close connection to the goddess.

Kobie's growl was all the warning Mellaia had to straighten and back away from Duella's side.

He vaulted to the bedside and snatched the heart stone from his son's chest. Duella's defensive movement didn't escape his attention.

Does he beat her? Does he berate her? The latter was almost a given, the former less certain.

Mellaia didn't have time to question it.

In the next moment, Kobie moved from sacrilege to atrocity by placing the stone over his own heart. As it had with his son, the stone glowed weakly.

One of her attendants crept to the doorway, then bolted away. The rest left their ceremonial places and gathered around her.

Mellaia bit back a shudder. *Why did I insist Grom stop hovering over me? I should have known better than to come here, of all places, without his protection.*

Kobie glared at Mellaia, holding the stone so hard his knuckles were pale and the veins in his arm made ridges on the skin's surface. "What have you done to it?" he demanded.

She stiffened her spine, noting that Kobie was significantly shorter than Grom was in amusement. *He is trying to frighten me, but I have ceased to be afraid of Grom's men. Even if he dares touch me, Grom will kill him for it.*

Her lack of reaction seemed to confuse him, but Kobie recovered quickly. "I asked —"

Artell stepped between them, closing the circle of protection, her claws loosed and her hair standing on edge. "*I* prepared the stone, in the precise manner it has always been done."

His face darkened and fur sprouted on his hands, though he reined in his claws. "It has been tampered with," he insisted. "She has done something to —"

Mellaia snapped. "There is nothing I could do to sway the heart stone. Monnan alone speaks through it."

"Liar!"

Artell gasped. "You dare?"

"Kobie, no." Duella went wide-eyed, her color dipping in a manner that made Mellaia fear she would need the services of a healer.

Kobie wasn't finished yet. "When I was a babe, I pulsed hot."

"Perhaps Monnan no longer finds you worthy," Mellaia countered.

He threw the stone against the wall so hard, the nerve-wracking sound of cracking filled the chamber. It went spinning away to the far corner.

Everyone stared at him in apparent shock. Before Mellaia composed herself to confront him, Artell started speaking.

"Let me guess, Kobie." She struck a mocking pose, staring at her claws as if they were more important than he was. "Your *dame* told you that you pulsed with power."

He stepped toward them, glaring. Mellaia's sense of self-preservation told her to run.

Never give an enemy your back. She planted her feet and tilted her head up proudly.

"Are you calling my dame a liar?" His voice was cold and uncompromising, a challenge woven into the demand.

Mellaia slid her hand into her pocket, closing it around the ceremonial dagger, preparing to defend herself.

"You're calling my dame a *liar.*" His fangs descended into place.

"Get out!" Duella shouted. The new dame trembled in anger.

Kobie shot her a look of disbelief.

Mellaia tipped her head in agreement, preparing to withdraw. *With my apologies. A new dame should not be so stressed. She should have peace to settle in with her babes.*

Duella didn't look at her. She glowered at her mate, seemingly seething.

Mellaia hesitated. *Is she demanding he take action to make us leave? Is she angry with him and not us?*

"I told you to leave me, Kobie."

Evio fussed, and Duella repositioned him to her shoulder without moving her gaze from Kobie.

He pasted on a smile that turned Mellaia's stomach. "Duella...you are—"

"Well beyond tired of your games. Mortified to be associated with you. Sick of the sight and sound of you. Get. Out!"

Kobie straightened, scowling down at her. "Duella—"

She loosed her teeth and claws, her muzzle appearing in a flash. A deep, rumbling growl made Mellaia shiver in awareness.

Why has she let Kobie lord over her? She is stronger than he. Especially now that she is protectress to her young.

Something else niggled at her thoughts. *She's issuing a warning to Kobie. Duella feels the need to protect their young from him.*

Kobie opened his mouth to speak.

Grom's voice stepped up the tension in the chamber. "You heard the female clearly enough, Kobie. I *suggest* you comply with Duella's wishes."

"She is my *mate*," he grumbled. Kobie didn't turn to face Grom when he addressed him.

He's dismissing Grom. He is showing disrespect to my mate. *To his prince.* The back of her neck burned in anger.

"That is for Duella to decide, when she feels equal to making such a decision." Grom strode further into the chamber, planting himself between the priestesses and attendants and their shared foe.

Between me and Kobie. I knew he would protect me. Mellaia loosened her grip on the dagger, letting it settle further into the pocket of her robes, relieved.

Kobie whipped toward him. "And where am I to rest but with my mate?"

Broll, Bevor, and other guards Mellaia recognized took up protective positions around the throng of women. One of them moved to Duella's side.

In the event that Kobie turns on her.

"I will leave," Duella offered. She'd taken her fully-human form again, and she appeared worn to exhaustion.

Kobie went pale. "No. Stay. I would...prefer you to stay in comfort. I will bunk with the unmated men, for the time being."

As long as she stays, Kobie is providing for her.

As if confirming it, Kobie continued. "I will send meat and milk down to you."

Duella was silent for a potent moment, and Kobie tensed in response.

"I would appreciate it. Until my dame arrives to aid me," she hastened to qualify.

Kobie darkened, a sure sign that he wanted Duella's dame nowhere near her.

"I will send for her immediately," Grom vowed.

A low growl rumbled between them, and Kobie tried to glare Grom down. He failed, of course.

Kobie composed himself. "As you wish, Duella. Sleep well." With that, he stomped his way out of the chamber and disappeared from view.

Grom didn't turn to Mellaia immediately. He tipped his head to Duella. "If there is anything you require, you have only to ask. If you would feel safer with guards —"

"Please," she blurted out, seemingly at the edges of tears.

"Your dame resides...?"

"In Rowlen." Duella managed a weak smile at that, and Mellaia wondered if she would choose to return there with her dame.

"My shuttle will deliver her within the day."

She stared at him, apparently at a loss for words.

"Sleep well, little cousin."

She nodded, then startled at a deep growl.

Mellaia glared at the male responsible, a rebuke dying in her throat at the sight of him holding the fractured stone.

It's gone. Destroyed. If it's the only one, how will our babes be introduced to Monnan's light.

"I am truly sorry for the loss of the stone," Duella intoned.

"It was not your doing," Mellaia assured her. She reached out for the stone, and the male settled it carefully in her hands.

Were it not for the fact that the heart stone was surely ruined, the cracks' design would have been pretty. As it was, cradling it and fighting back tears was the most positive response she could manage.

Grom appeared at her side, stroking a hand up and down her arm in soothing. "All will be well. We have several. That one was simply the traditional stone."

She breathed a sigh of relief. *But they may not test evenly. We may not have another usable stone.* She resolved not to say that aloud. Duella already blamed herself for the loss of the stone.

"Mellaia?" Grom prompted her.

"With Duella's permission, I would like to use each stone to test her babes. That will allow me to choose the successor stone."

"For *calibration*?" he asked.

She shook her head, at a loss to put that term in context she could understand.

"To learn which test similarly?"

"Yes." *Not quite, but close enough.*

"It would be my honor," Duella decided. "But...if you would excuse me now, I am fatigued."

She looked it. Her face had gone nearly colorless. Mellaia felt her protective urges swell, like a ripple beneath her skin.

"Of course. We will withdraw," she assured the new dame.

Grom started to lead her away. "Zhabin and Rellen. It is your watch."

Everyone split in the corridors, heading their own ways. When she and Grom were alone, he started asking questions of her.

"Why did he smash the stone?"

"Because he and his son both tested poorly."

Grom scowled. "He has held a grudge over his testing all this time?"

"It seems his dame told him he'd tested well. From what Artell said, I take it that is not unheard of."

He shot her a look that postulated on more.

Mellaia sighed. "He accused... He believes I've tampered with the heart stone somehow. But I cannot have."

"It is impossible," he agreed.

Grom was lost in brooding silence for a moment. Just when Mellaia would have questioned him, he spoke again.

"Go nowhere alone...or even in the sole company of females. If I cannot be by your side, there will be guards."

"I would suggest the same for Artell. Kobie wants her blood."

"It will be done."

* * * *

Duella took the platter of meat from Zhabin's hands, and Mellaia bit back a smile. She'd spoken with Duella several times in the days it took Derr to collect the stones from the far reaches of their world. Zhabin doted on Duella, so much so that Mellaia wondered if he might be intent on her as mate, should she ultimately refuse Kobie. She had deferred on that decision so far.

Mellaia chuckled at the sight of Elyss grabbing for the stone. "Another young female enchanted by the jewel."

"My mother says I was as well," Duella offered.

Dyanna made a sound that spoke of exasperation. "You tried to steal the testing stone every time you spied it."

Duella darkened at her mother's accusation, but she didn't dispute it. She dug into her meal while the babies were otherwise occupied.

Smart woman.

Mellaia laughed, letting Elyss hold her grip for a few moments. "I often took the heart stone on adventures with me. I believed the Goddess would like that."

She whispered the blessing, then touched the first stone to Elyss's chest. It sputtered weakly. Mellaia moved it to Evio's. The light wavered sickly, then went out. Duella winced.

"This stone is defective," Mellaia announced. Still, she handled it with reverence. It had once held Monnan's essence faithfully, else it would not have been consecrated.

"I hope there is a useable stone," Duella breathed. "If *he* destroyed the last, I will never forgive myself."

"It was not your doing," Mellaia repeated.

Zhabin turned her attention back to the waiting meal.

I will have to thank him for that later.

The second stone glowed but still not as brightly.

"Lower than the traditional stone. I hope for better."

The third shone strong on Elyss...then started pulsing slowly. Evio had a better showing than his first, but still muted in comparison to his sister.

"Much better." Mellaia felt the tension in her chest relax away. *We have a useable stone. Thank Monnan!* "Now for the last."

That stone gave a response nearly identical to the traditional stone.

"Perfect," Duella breathed. "It matches."

Mellaia wasn't as sure. *A stone loses essence over time. I hadn't considered finding a stronger stone. What if the traditional stone was wearing thin?*

"Is there a problem, Mellaia?" Dyanna asked.

"How long has the traditional stone been in use?" she inquired.

"Since the great quake. It was the first located in the rubble of the smaller southern temple."

"And the one in the main temple?"

"Was never found. That temple was lost to the chasm that opened beneath it."

As I thought. The one they've been using was an auxiliary stone. It wasn't even the secondary; there was a stronger stone.

"Mellaia?" Dyanna prompted her again.

"I would like to test each of us with the last two."

There was a moment of tense silence.

Mellaia sighed. "I believe... I believe the traditional stone had become weak over time. We all know how we tested...or nearly so. Typically, the strongest stone is used, at any rate, but I believe the other should have been replaced long ago."

"Do it," Duella urged her.

Since Duella was the youngest, Mellaia started with her. She tried the lesser stone first, and Dyanna confirmed it was a close match for Duella's original testing, a strong shine but not pulsing. The other stone pulsed strongly.

She repeated the process on Zhabin, with much the same results. Mellaia didn't miss the sideward glance Duella sent the young male, the blush that darkened her cheeks as she looked away.

So, he isn't the only one attracted.

Mellaia turned to Dyanna and repeated the process with the lesser stone. It glowed at a moderate level. She looked up at the older female.

Dyanna's brow was creased in seeming confusion. "I believe you may be correct. I was told I glowed strongly."

"I suspected as much. Now the other."

The stronger stone glowed brightly but did not pulse.

"That matches what my dame reported," she confirmed.

Mellaia's joy melted into a sobering reality.

Dyanna's smile disappeared. "Is there a problem?"

She cradled the stone, her mind working hard at the situation. "Duella said these were the last. Why has there been no attempt to mine new heart stones? Was the mine lost to the quakes?"

The two females stared at each other, then turned to her, dumbstruck.

Zhabin cleared his throat. "The stones do not originate on this world, Lady Mellaia. Sadly, the cataclysm that...took our priestesses from us also took their amassed knowledge of such from us. The only thing we know of the source is that it is called the World of the Biting Moon."

She winced at the thought, then realization stopped her cold. "*The Snow King*," she whispered in her native tongue.

"Pardon, Lady Mellaia?" he asked.

She gathered the stones, her head spinning.

"Mellaia?" Dyanna prompted her.

"I must speak with Grom." She rushed away with barely a tip of her head for the new dame, her guards in her wake.

* * * *

Grom vaulted to his feet at the sight of his mate barreling through the doorway. The hand movement from the head of her guards let him know all was well, and he took a calming breath.

Still, Mellaia's flushed appearance and distraction worried him. She arranged the testing stones on her work table, clearly lost in thought. Grom waved his men away to the corridor. Whatever this was, it might be a personal matter.

The moment they were gone, he went to her, drawing Mellaia into his arms. "What ails you?" Whatever it was, it would meet a decisive end.

"We must return to my world."

His blood ran cold. "What?" Was she dismissing him as a mate? What had happened in his absence? It seemed every time she left his side, something monumental happened.

"It is imperative. The stones—"

"You couldn't find a match?" He cursed the idea of them losing the last testing stone. How would their own young be tested?

"I found a usable stone."

Grom squeezed his eyes shut, thanking Monnan for her blessings silently.

"It is the last usable stone we have, and I estimate we have a generation. Two at the most, before that stone becomes as unusable as the others."

His heart stuttered at the truth of the matter. "Two generations, and then we lose Monnan's light." *I will be the last king with ties to the Goddess Dame.*

Mellaia turned to him, shaking her head, her color high. "You don't understand. The stones never came from your world."

81

"I know." He tried not to growl the words, failing horribly at the attempt. *If only we knew the world they came from.*

"Did it never occur to you that we also use heart stones on my world?"

Words failed him. Grom stared at her, his mind rioting.

"You assumed your missing crewmember brought the stone with him when he fled, but he did not, Grom. The stones come from *my* world. Your people came there to mine them, every ten or so generations. Our people also hunted together."

"How could you know this?" *What did I miss?*

"The Snow King."

Her foreign term confused him. "Pardon?"

She smiled, then led him to a lounging couch. Grom settled on it and drew her into his lap. Mellaia didn't hesitate.

"I thought it was a story, but it all fits. When I met you, I called you a son of Luna...Monnan. You remember?"

He nodded.

"There was a story we used to tell at mid-winter festival. It spoke of visitors...Sons of Luna. They appeared every ten generations, at the height of winter. They would spend two moons with us, choose the strongest of our males to go into the mines with them, and the two tribes would part, each with new heart stones. Before the visitors left, our people would hunt together and share a great feast. The highest ranking son of Luna would be hailed as the Snow King.

"Many generations ago, they...*you* stopped coming. Our males would collect the stones without them, at the appointed time, and we would feast in celebration. I don't know why I never questioned it before now, but until Zhabin mentioned—"

"Mentioned what?" *If he caused this upset—*

"He said your people called the world the World of the Biting Moon."

Grom nodded at the term she'd used.

"My people call the cold, winter moon the Biting Moon."

He drew in a deep breath, stunned by the realization. "Why is it called the Biting Moon?"

"That is less clear, but the stories say the first Snow King shared blood with the first Mistress."

"You believe the first Mistress was one of our people."

"I would have, but..." She worked her lip between her teeth, seemingly considering something of greatest importance.

"Yes?"

She cuddled into his arms. "Remember my drive to bite you in return?"

Grom nodded.

"I believe the first Mistress was from my tribe, but that she and the first Snow King *literally* shared their blood, by way of...biting."

It made sense. Mellaia had gone into the mating frenzy, a frenzy she claimed was not natural to her people, after he claimed her with his bite. *Did we materially change her people in such a manner?*

Mellaia hurried on. "We must return to my world. Don't you see? We must gather new stones."

"Now? No. Our babes must be—"

She laughed. "No. Not now." Mellaia closed her eyes, looking serene. "I think we should plan our return for the traditional time."

"When would that be?"

"Does the trip back take the same amount of time as the trip to your world did?"

"It would be faster by half a moon if we went six moons later into the year."

She hummed a satisfied note. "I thought so. That would match with when the Sons of Luna had traditionally arrived on my world. They traveled at the time most suited to the trip."

"Agreed. We will travel at the next alignment."

Chapter Eleven

There was no mistaking the sensation of active labor. Mellaia pressed a fist to the wall, gritting her teeth as the pain ripped through her, much stronger than the earlier ones.

Zella stopped two steps further down the corridor, still speaking, as she turned back to look for Mellaia. Her smile faded, and her face went pale. "Dear Monnan! Artell, it is time."

The pain released her, and Mellaia took a deep breath. Her mate's mother and sister guided her to the sanctuary. Along the way, they ordered servants away to collect the healer, Grom, and Derr.

The chamber had been prepared for her weeks in advance. Before she could orientate herself, they'd stripped off her dress, then they helped her onto the low, padded mistress's prayer bed. Mellaia knelt up on the cushion, grasping the smooth, wooden bars at either side for balance.

She sucked in another deep breath as the pain returned, then tipped her head back, basking in Monnan's light, panting her way through the next contraction.

Artell kneaded the knotted muscles in her shoulders and back, while Zella massaged a calming oil into her abdomen. The dame paused with her hand beneath the bulge.

"She is laboring hard. More strenuously than I would have thought possible."

Artell rubbed harder. "Should I bring the *bluket*?"

Mellaia shook her head. "Not now. I will sick it up, for certain." Her stomach roiled at the thought of eating or drinking anything.

Artell hesitated. "But, Mellaia—"

"I had *bluket*." She groaned. "I had it earlier."

Silence fell as she took another deep breath at the release of pain. Mellaia looked at Grom's dame. The older female stared over her shoulder.

Most likely at Artell.

Then she shifted her focus to Mellaia. "Earlier? When?"

"Earlier in the labor," she qualified in return.

"How *much* earlier?"

"A quarter cycle ago. My hunger and thirst fled shortly afterward."

"Artell, get the healer," Zella ordered. "Get her now!"

The younger woman bolted from the chamber.

"Mellaia..." Zella faltered, pressed a hand to her forehead, composed herself, then began again. "Why would you labor in silence and solitude?"

The question made no sense. "I was not in solitude and silence. I have been in your company and Artell's for —"

"Why did you say nothing?" the dame demanded.

"What should I have said?" Whatever it was, clearly Grom had never told her about it.

"Why did you not tell us you were laboring? Why did you not make your pain clear to us?"

Mellaia shook her head, at a loss to understand her insistence and upset. "Why would I? Until the birth is close, there is nothing to be done." *Or perhaps it is not so in their kind.* She opened her mouth to ask it.

"How close?" Zella's expression said she feared something Mellaia had yet to discover for herself. "Can you tell?"

The next pain came abruptly, giving Mellaia no time to prepare. Mellaia gripped the bars, swallowing a cry of surprise. She squeezed her eyes shut, concentrating on the calm her grandmother had taught bearing women to use in labor for generations.

"Too close," Zella muttered. She went to work, massaging Mellaia's back as Artell had been doing.

A gush of fluid accompanied an increase in pain, and Mellaia gave in to the need to cry out in response to it.

* * * *

His dame's curse brought Grom up short. He stepped into the sanctuary just in time to see her drop to her knees on the floor, pushing her full sleeves back.

"Dame Zella?" he called out, confused by the urgency of her motions.

"Quickly, Grom."

Zella's hand disappeared into his mate's body, and Mellaia whimpered, a tear sliding down her cheek.

He vaulted across the chamber, then smoothed Mellaia's hair. His assessment was not reassuring. His mate cried out, her abdomen undulating in ways that made him queasy in sympathy.

"What is this?" he asked.

"The first of your young," Zella answered calmly.

"The f... Dear Monnan! Where is the healer?" Why had no one called for him earlier? The copper taste of true fear flooded his mouth.

"Help her, Grom. The first is descending."

Mellaia's panting ended abruptly, and she grunted in pain. Sweat coated her body and dripped from her temple to her cheek. Her muscles tightened down a few notches.

Grom slid onto the mistress's prayer bed behind her, while his dame circled them and knelt in the healer's usual spot. He slipped his legs between hers to force them wide, then he wrapped his arms around her and eased Mellaia to sitting on his thighs, positioning her to deliver. That accomplished, he started massaging her womb.

Her legs tightened against his; she trembled, most likely in the exertion of labor. Her fluids soaked through his trousers, and tears and sweat splashed onto his hands.

She sagged against him, her breathing ragged. Her hands loosened against the railings.

"It is a big one, but descending well," Zella reported.

"Soon," Grom whispered into his mate's hair. "You are doing well."

Her sob and stiffening body announced her struggle had resumed. Over and over, she pushed and released. Zella tended to her, at first alone and then with Artell's assistance.

Finally, the healer arrived. She ordered Artell to take over on the massage of Mellaia's womb, leaving Grom free to stimulate stronger contractions with nipple massage.

"Better," the healer decided. "They will pass quickly now."

True to her word, the healer handed off the first babe to Dame Zella only moments later.

"A female," his dame reported. She gasped, her eyes going wide and wild.

"What is it?" Grom barked the words more than spoke them.

"Her eyes."

He stared at her, demanding an answer silently.

"They are...purple. Soft blue-purple. Not unlike the light Mellaia makes when she touches the altar in the temple."

"A sign from the Goddess," he breathed. *Surely, our eldest is intended to be heir.*

"Perhaps."

The time to discuss it was not at hand, and discussion would not prove or disprove it.

The second came faster, a blessing considering Mellaia's exhaustion.

"A male," Artell informed them. "He has your eyes, Grom."

His dame's bid to win the wagers came crashing to ground when the third started descending. "Damn the luck," she grumbled. "Thirteen cycles and nearly nine bluestone, but there are more than two."

It was probably best that Mellaia required his full attention. Otherwise, he might have snapped at his dame. The wagers were amusing while his mate was not suffering for them. They had ceased to be so the first time Mellaia had given voice to a full-throated scream of pain. That scream had frayed his nerves worse than emergencies in deep space and battle combined had.

Mellaia's thighs tightened against his, and the unmistakable feel of a child sliding along his trousers announced their third babe's entry into Monnan's light.

"No more," she begged. "No more, please."

Grom made soothing noises, grooming her sweat-soaked and tangled hair. There was no vow he could make her in good conscience. He couldn't promise that this was the last when there might be more babes coming. Neither could he promise her that it was almost over; not when the next might take as long as the first had.

"A male," Derr announced.

I have no memory of my sire arriving. That was a galling thing for a warrior to admit to himself.

I have more important concerns. "And his eyes?" Grom asked.

"Green as your dame's."

Grom turned his attention to the healer. "Are there more?"

She smiled weakly. "Thank Monnan, no. It is nearly over now."

Mellaia whimpered as the cord base passed, then sighed in relief, going boneless in his arms.

The next few moments slid away in near silence. The healer nodded to let him know that Mellaia was well. The birthing quilt was brought forward; Grom wrapped Mellaia in it, then lifted her into his arms.

The procession to their rooms passed in a blur. Grom offered a few strained smiles and nods to the servants who knelt in doorways, hoping to be among the first to sight and scent Grom's young. Most of his attention went to his exhausted mate and the three bundled babes carried by his family members.

Their rooms never looked so appealing to him, and he ordered the door closed behind them.

* * * *

Mellaia awoke to the sensation of a tiny hand patting her breast. A huff of dissatisfaction followed, and she opened her eyes.

The babe demanding her attention had a head full of her sire's dark curls.

Not a hint of my red. At least not yet. Babes were known to darken or lighten in hair color as they grew.

Mellaia didn't question which child it was. As Zella had described her daughter's eyes as being temple purple, and neither of her sons shared the color, which other child could it be?

Mellaia turned toward her, enjoying the first, quiet moments of bonding with her babe.

The oldest of my children, but the others will seek my attention when they have need of it.

Another slap against her breast and a screwed-up countenance announced the babe would not be happy with another delay in procuring a meal. Mellaia positioned the closer nipple, smiling as nuzzling led to avid feasting. Before she quite knew what she intended, she found herself murmuring a lullaby.

Grom came into the room, one of their sons snug against his chest. He stopped and smiled, then ambled toward them, rapt on the vision of her feeding their daughter.

"Does he require a feeding as well?" she asked.

"He does not seem to, at the moment, but the scent of your milk may change that." Grom settled on the edge of the bed, stroking a finger along their daughter's arm "Have you decided on names?"

"She...is Issah."

His smile widened. "Issah. Beautiful."

"It was my dame's name."

"Will one of our sons be named for your sire?"

"I will have to meet them before I make such a decision." She added a note of teasing to her words, and he laughed in response.

The babe in his arms started to fuss.

"He's smelled the milk," she noted.

"Then perhaps you should meet him."

Grom supported their son to allow her to feed him without changing position. He latched on with no assistance from Mellaia. After a moment, he looked up and met her gaze.

Our older son. He has Grom's eyes.

"Will he have your sire's name?" Grom asked.

"No. His name is...Groll."

"A strong name," he mused.

They sat in silence while Issah and Groll engaged in their first meal. When Issah was done, Grom placed their son in her spot and burped their daughter. He handled her as if he'd cared for babes for years.

He looked up at her, paused, then sighed. "I was overjoyed when Artell had young. I spent as much time as possible caring for them."

"I look forward to your aid," she assured him.

His smile returned, and he leaned to place a kiss on her lips. Grom lingered, and she savored his touch.

Groll released her breast, and Grom drew away and straightened. He stared down at their son in disbelief, then looked down at himself.

Mellaia followed his line of sight, gasping at the thin line of blood rolling down his abdomen. Before she could question him, Grom started laughing hard.

"Certainly a sign from the Goddess."

"Groll did *that*?" she questioned, horrified.

"He is... There is a word for it, among your people. I found it once."

"Jealous?" she offered.

"Yes. Jealous. You are his dame. He wishes you for himself."

"He won't—"

"Attack his brother and sister? Highly unlikely. And you..." He cupped a hand beneath her chin. "You are not to worry about me. I expected a certain amount of animosity from our young. He will learn quickly enough that I am not a competitor for your love and care."

His words warmed her heart. He was going to be a wonderful sire.

As if responding to the fact that her breasts were available for a meal, their younger son started to squall from another chamber. Zella entered with him, bringing the babe to the bed.

Mellaia turned, putting the opposite breast into the feeding position. For all the noise he made, he was in no hurry to sample the milk. He stared up at her, reaching a hand for her face. She leaned down and kissed him, smiling as he grabbed a handful of her hair and pulled it to his mouth.

"If you are hungry, I have better for you," she whispered.

Their son continued to stare at her, patiently waiting for something she couldn't name.

This is not my sire. A memory stirred in her.

"Hareem," she decided.

"Your sire's name?" Grom guessed.

"No. My dame's sire. He was a patient man, just as young Hareem is."

As if he was showing approval of his name, Hareem released her hair, turned toward her, then started to feed.

Zella took Issah, making odd little sounds to the babe that she seemed to thrive on. At a break in her repertoire, she glanced at the rest of the family, lounging together on the bed. "Have you named them all?" she asked.

Grom nodded. "Issah is in your arms. Groll is here with me, and Hareem, as you heard, is feeding well."

Her brow went up. "And which of them has taken offense to your continued living?" she teased.

"Groll," Mellaia supplied. At Zella's contemplation, Mellaia felt her heart start to pound. "What is it?" she asked.

"I had wagered on Issah as chosen heir, but now I wonder whether I should have wagered on Groll."

Derr appeared in the doorway. "My bluestone is on Groll. It would not do to have us on the same side of the wager." His smile was nothing short of sexual in nature. "After all, how would we settle our *personal* wager?"

Zella shot him a quelling look. "Persist, and you will find me a most unwinnable wager." Her teeth flashed, a clear warning for her mate.

Grom reached out and took Issah from his dame's outstretched arms. Zella sauntered out of the chamber, and Derr followed in her wake, single-minded in his pursuit of her. Grom waited until they were out of sight, then roared in laughter.

Mellaia stroked a hand through Hareem's hair, noting the red highlights glimmering in the dim light. "And who would you wager on?" she asked her mate.

"You."

She laughed. "Amongst our children?"

"Whichever is most like you." He settled behind her, laying a kiss on her shoulder. "Of course, I will have to meet them all to be certain."

Chapter Twelve

Mellaia lay on the mistress's prayer bed, cushioned by lush pillows, covered by soft blankets, and surrounded by her babes.

The crowd was larger than she'd expected, males and females dressed in all manner of finery. Duella sat in a comfortable chair placed at the front of the amassed guests. She held Elyss, and Zhabin held Evio. Dyanna wrapped a light blanket around Duella's legs.

Artell stepped forward, wearing the robes of a lesser priestess. She opened her mouth to start the song of introduction.

Kobie spoke, rudely interrupting the proceedings. "Excuse me, my king, but is this *proper*?"

All around him, people glared at him. More than likely, they knew he'd tried to destroy the heart stone. His very presence in this place was nothing short of sacrilege.

Before Mellaia could counter the accusation, Derr did. "Artell is a priestess, and she has been trained to test new young."

"But a royal testing for who shall lead next?" he continued, heedless that half the chamber wanted him dead.

Duella threw off the blanket and handed her daughter to Dyanna. She strode toward the altar, and reached her hand out toward Artell. The latter handed over the heart stone with a faint smile.

Kobie stared at her, wild-eyed.

"I am in training," she offered. "I started within days of my babes' birth. I am trained far enough to test young. If you find it repugnant that Artell should do her sacred duty, I shall do mine." The set of her jaw dared him to protest.

He seemed to consider it carefully. Finally, Kobie backed away with a tip of his head. Something in his expression chilled Mellaia, and she gathered the blankets around her babes in response.

Duella and Artell sang together, Artell leading the way when Duella was unsure of the cadence. When the song ended, she approached the bed.

"Name your young, Mellaia," she requested.

"My daughter is Issah. My elder son is Groll. My younger son is Hareem."

"Issah, so named, know the touch of our goddess, Monnan."

She settled the stone on Issah's chest. It glowed brightly enough to make the eyes ache and started to pulse. A roar of approval went up around the room.

"First chosen," Duella shouted. "Issah, daughter of Grom and Mellaia."

The sounds tapered off, and Duella retrieved the stone Issah was attempting to chew on. She wiped it reverently.

"Groll, so named, know the touch of our goddess, Monnan."

The stone shone brightly, but not as brightly as it had with Issah. It pulsed slower, but pulse it did.

"Second chosen," Duella announced. "Groll, son of Grom and Mellaia."

The crowd went wild at the pronouncement. It took them longer to settle that time.

Duella prepared the stone again. "Hareem, so named, know the touch of our goddess, Monnan."

The stone glowed strongly, but it did not pulse.

"A fine, strong son," she complimented Mellaia.

The crowd let loose in howls.

Grom leaned close to whisper in Mellaia's ear. "The formal welcome to the pack."

She smiled. The smile faded at the sight of Kobie staring at her. His eyes were narrowed, his stance stiff.

The back of her neck radiated heat, a scorching discomfort that made her heart pound.

Whatever his plan is, it is coming soon.

* * * *

The attack, though expected, was no less nerve wracking when it happened. Sounds of snapping and snarling, crashes and yelps of pain broke the silence around them.

Artell vaulted across the room, clearing the bed in a single jump. She helped Mellaia move the babes to the padded enclosure at the far side of the room.

Groll let loose a low growl, and Mellaia soothed him.

I have to soothe him. I want their focus on us, *not on the children. If they make it this far.*

"He is entirely too bold," Artell grumbled.

"You honestly expected Kobie to attack when Grom and Broll were here?" *We are never unguarded, but better facing Grom's guards than Grom himself, and Duella's summons for Kobie to dismiss him would mean royal intervention.* "He had to know this was his only chance at us."

A yelp of pain and the copper scent of blood attested that the fighting was fierce. A chilling crash of wood ended in silence that made Mellaia's ears ache in its absoluteness.

In a flash, Artell had partially shifted, then placed herself between Mellaia and any enemies remaining. Nearly as quickly, three males pounced from the shadow of the doorway, in their wariken forms; they piled on her, driving Artell to the floor beneath their bulk.

Artell didn't submit to them. Rather, she went for throats. She tore out the first, sending a spray of blood across the bed linens.

The second was less sloppy in defense; the best Artell could manage was a pawful of deep claw marks that laid bare his cheek and took one eye. The male pushed away from her, whining in a most unrefined manner, then fled the chamber.

The final warrior was not as weak as his brother warriors were. In a matter of moments, he had her pinned to the floor, both wrists locked behind her back, captured in his now-human hands, her split lip letting loose rivulets of blood down her chin.

In walked Kobie, fully unruffled.

He lets others do the fighting for him. Coward.

"Stop fighting me or I will kill you," the male restraining Artell ordered.

The itching and burning at the back of Mellaia's neck and scalp gained momentum. *A little late, are you not?* she asked bitterly.

"Remember what I said," Kobie addressed his fellow traitor. "Render her unconscious if you must. Do not kill her. Artell is the one we need."

"*You* need," he snapped back. "Though heirs from the *former* ruling family would be a boon, I have no need for them."

Mellaia's mouth went dry. *Former? Grom and Derr are not dead. I do not believe they are both gone. He lies.* She tightened her grip on the ceremonial blade, fiery determination driving her.

"*We,*" Kobie countered patiently. "With Artell to finish training Duella, we will both have what we want. A return to the glory days of our forefathers."

Her entire body itched, as if her skin was too tight, her anger making ripples that readied her muscles for a fight. Kobie stepped into range, and she struck, planting the blade in his throat, then ripping it free with a twist to bleed him fast.

Even if his healing keeps him alive — unlikely as that is — he will not be able to continue fighting this day.

Her vision sharpened, and Mellaia watched him die, satisfied with her performance. She stood over him, straight and proud, while he gurgled and coughed, drowning in his own blood. He fell, twitching and clawing at the floor.

"You should have gone where you were bid," she informed him. *You would have been banished from the royal city, dismissed by your former mate, but you would have been alive to find a new mate and true happiness someday.*

A growl from the doorway brought Mellaia's attention to the injured wariken guard facing off with Artell's captor. The traitor male laid a blow to Artell's head that made her go limp mid-swing toward him. She crumpled beneath him, and the guard charged at his foe. They met halfway, clashing hard, though the scrappy, young wariken was significantly smaller than his opponent.

The urge to drag Artell from the fight, lest she be injured further by them, warred with the instructions she'd given Mellaia weeks ago.

"Do not let them draw you out, Mellaia. Stand your ground between your young and the traitors; do not allow them to pass you to do harm to the babes. Delay them until our men arrive to gut them. Pray our guards are enough and Grom is swift."

So far my prayers have not yielded positive results. Only my actions have. Still, she held her ground, trusting to Artell's vast experience at fighting her own kind. *The traitor did not kill her; perhaps he feels Kobie's plan is sound, that he will need a priestess to hold power. My babes need* me.

The battle went on longer than Mellaia had anticipated it would. In the end, the result was precisely as she'd expected it would pass. The guard lay, battered and bleeding, trying desperately to rise, despite his injuries.

He returned to his human form, rising from a crouch. He was injured but not incapacitated, a formidable male who was nearly Grom's height and width. Strangely, she found him less than imposing.

The burning subsided to a stroke of awareness along her skin. Mellaia found herself calm in the face of her adversary, certain he would fail to pass her.

"It would be dishonorable to kill you as a wariken," he informed her. "Therefore, I will kill you in this...*weakened* form."

"You bring me to my knees."

I am Grom's mate, chosen by Monnan Herself to be his, to be the leader's woman. Grom bows *to me.* "You think I am *weak*?"

"I know you are." He started toward her, seemingly intent on her end.

Mine and my babes after me. Fury ignited, a stream of hate riding her veins.

Groll growled, and Issah followed suit. His eyes narrowed, and he tilted his head to one side, as if he could see the babes behind her.

The blade dropped from her numb fingers, and the heat bloomed outward to the tips of her fingers and toes.

His smile melted into a look of horror. The next moment was a flurry of fur and sound...and of blood. Screams echoed off the walls and one of her young howled.

* * * *

Grom cursed solidly in his mind, snapping the leg of one of Kobie's fighters. He used the opening when the wariken shied away to rip him open from throat to hips, then left him in his wake.

What in Monnan's name did he promise them? He would guess a return to the dark times before the testing, when they lost many a good fighter in battles for leadership, a war whenever a leader aged or sickened. *Or just because another strong male took a dislike to the leader in power.* Endless infighting and bloodshed. At least the testing had limited the number of contenders to the rare few who pulsed with power. Even then, it had been a hand of generations since the last test of fang and claw.

I could guess it, but Kobie would never rule in such a system. No one would follow him as leader, and putting himself in service to another leader does not sound like something Kobie would do.

Another traitor attacked, and Grom flipped him to his back and took his throat. He moved steadily toward the chambers where Mellaia and their young were no doubt under siege.

I underestimated Kobie. I thought he would find only a few willing to support his madness.

Did I assign enough guards? The fur at his hackles stiffened in frustration. Not knowing was maddening.

Two more wariken darted in from his left, and Grom whipped their direction, prepared to prove his place as heir yet again. He stopped short of taking another throat at the sight and scent of Derr and Broll.

Artell is with Mellaia. If their young are safe with Dame Zella, Broll will want to secure his mate.

Grom turned and loped away, the others at his heels. At the sight of the three of them moving as a unit, wariken who might have tested Grom alone fled in terror.

They will pay the price later. Every one of them.

With no remaining resistance, they crossed the distance in moments. A growl built in his throat at the downed guards littering the corridor and the visiting chamber. He laid on speed at the sound of tense voices.

Female. He wanted to believe one of them was Mellaia, but he couldn't differentiate, as low as they were speaking.

Growls and howls let him know those inside were under attack, and he launched into the fray...then halted in shock.

The victim of the attack was a male in human form. The rest confused him. The female was half-shifted into wariken form, but it wasn't Artell attacking. His sister was unconscious on the floor. Before Grom turned his head away, he saw Broll scoop her to his chest, murmuring her name.

The scene before him was even more vicious when he returned his attention to it. The female had ripped out his throat already, and she was still savaging her adversary, tearing at his chest and arms, growling, her fangs dripping with thick blood.

The swirl of green and purple left no doubt as to who the female was.

"Mellaia."

She threw her head back and howled a war cry that their young echoed. Then she pushed to her feet, meeting his eyes solidly.

Grom had hardly enough time to marvel at the beauty of her black-red pelt before the shift slid over her. He shifted to human form, searching for words with which to address her with little success.

Mellaia weaved on her feet, reaching for the table to steady herself. He gathered her to his body, thanking Monnan silently for preserving his mate and young for him.

Blinding light rose around them, pulsing in dizzying circles until it coalesced into the image of one of the wolves from her world, howling at a full moon. The image continued to pulse, seemingly a living, breathing representation of the animal. Grom looked down at her, gaping at the sight of her holding the shattered testing stone in her hand.

"It pulses when it's nowhere near your heart," he noted.

Mellaia nodded weakly, and Grom lifted her and placed her on the side of the bed opposite where Broll had laid Artell. Before he'd had a chance to pull the blankets over her, she was half asleep.

"Sire?" he called out.

"Yes?" Derr straightened, leaving the last of their living guards laying in a pool of his own blood.

"We need healers."

"Done."

"We are missing one of the guards," Broll reported. "Did a traitor help them reach our mates?"

"Find him," Grom ordered.

"He is missing half his face," Mellaia reported under her breath.

Grom felt his fangs lengthen. "Find. Him."

First he will die, then every traitor who backed Kobie will join him.

Every Wolkin royal, from the days of testing to the present, had vowed not to relive the days when the streets ran red with the blood of warring armies for the throne.

Kobie broke that truce, and now all who aided him will pay the price. For Mellaia. For my young. For the future of our world.

Chapter Thirteen

Mellaia smoothed her gown, willing her wriggling stomach to still. They'd come so far, and the chance of failure still stalked her.

I must convince them. Our people depend on it.

The irony that she'd come to think of the Wolkin as her people wasn't lost on her. The oddity of greeting her grandmother as an equal was even more disconcerting.

Grom emerged from the bathing chamber, dressed in finery befitting his station—purple and gold as he always wore, but this outfit included a long-sleeved shirt and hide boots, lined with soft fur. It occurred to her that she'd never seen Grom in foot coverings before.

He smiled at her, then circled her body as if he was inspecting her choice of clothing. Mellaia turned to him, staring him down, challenging the presumption.

He bows to me.

Grom laughed, then leaned and kissed her forehead. "I was just thinking..."

"Yes?" At the note of teasing in his voice, Mellaia relaxed.

"There is one more thing you should wear."

She looked down at herself, confused by that pronouncement. "There is?"

He went to the cabinet, humming a note she couldn't decipher. When he returned, there was a delicate chain trailing from his hand. Mellaia looked at it, wondering at the use of something so fragile.

Grom looped the chain around her neck, settling the broken heart stone in the center of her chest. Since it wasn't skin-to-skin with her, it didn't erupt into searing light as it would if she touched it.

Mellaia swallowed hard, torn.

"What is it?" Grom asked.

"It is a beautiful gift, but..."

He cocked his head to one side, a brow rising in silent question.

"Will it be seen as sacrilegious?"

His smile returned, then widened. "No one else has the effect on the stones you do. Monnan has chosen you to wear this stone. I believe that."

His praise made her blush. At a loss for how to answer him, Mellaia went up on tiptoe and kissed him.

Grom dragged her closer, into a heated kiss. Since she'd fully recovered from childbirth, he'd been nearly insatiable.

As have I.

The door opened, and someone half-swallowed laughter. Grom didn't back off, which meant Mellaia would have to. She extricated herself from his embrace, offering him a silent promise of finishing once the formalities had been attended to.

Then she turned toward the doorway, offering a smile to Duella. She was surrounded by three toddling babes, all dressed in finery—Issah and Groll in heir's colors and Hareem in noble red.

How quickly Wolkin young mature. A babe at their age, born in the village, would still be carried in furs on a mother's back or in a nursing sling.

Grom's hands closed on her shoulders, and his tension was impossible to miss. Mellaia bit back a sigh, certain she knew what he was thinking.

"Are you certain?" he asked for the third time.

She managed a strained smile. "I am."

"Very well."

She loved that he didn't question her, though she was more than a little nervous. *We will follow the stories. Grandmother Joffa will recognize what our appearance means.*

They made their way through the corridors of the ship, Grom carrying Issah and holding Hareem's hand, Mellaia holding Groll's. At the top of the ramp, each of them donned a silken cape to keep them warm in the winter air.

Fighters from the village were already amassed, in a tense stand-off with the Wolkin guards. Each guard in human form was partnered by one in wariken, though the villagers would believe the latter were larger-than-usual wolves, trained to fight alongside their handlers.

They descended the ramp as a family, leaving Duella behind, Zhabin guarding his mate. Halfway down, there was movement at the back of the group of fighters. Mellaia's grandmother pushed her way through, ordering them to stand down. Joffa reached the Wolkin guards, and they closed ranks to block her.

"Let her through," Mellaia told them in her own language.

At her request, Grom had outfitted all their guards with translator cuffs to allow them to listen to the villagers and to allow the villagers to understand what commands she gave.

To their credit, the guards didn't so much as look back at her for confirmation. They parted to let her grandmother through.

She met them at the foot of the ramp, throwing her arms around Mellaia with a sound halfway between a laugh and a sob. Joffa shook so hard, it almost seemed she'd abruptly succumbed to a withering palsey.

Out of the corner of her eye, Mellaia saw their guards tense; the village warriors did the same. Grom ordered their own to calm, and — again — the villagers followed their lead.

Would that it will continue thus.

Joffa pulled back to look Mellaia in the face. "I thought you were lost forever."

"No. Simply..." She glanced at Grom and smiled, then returned her attention to the old woman. "The magic you gave me worked far better than we'd anticipated."

At the mention of the man Monnan had called for her, her grandmother raked an assessing gaze down Grom's body, then back up again. "A fine-looking male," she concluded.

Not to be outdone, Groll grasped his great-grandmother's skirt and yanked, demanding attention.

She smiled sweetly at the child. "And what would *your* name be?"

Grom dusted off the greeting she'd taught him. Though his inflection was odd, he dutifully reproduced the words, just as she had when greeting his parents.

"It is my honor to greet you, Mistress Joffa. May I present a gift of friendship?"

She seemed taken aback by the offer, even looking to Mellaia for counsel. At her nod, her grandmother managed a stiff smile.

"You may."

Grom released Hareem's hand, and the youngster toddled to Joffa and took a handful of her skirt in his hand, laying claim to an adult of his own. In the meantime, her mate retrieved the cuff from his pouch and reached for her.

"And what name may I address you by?" Joffa asked.

He clipped the cuff on her ear before answering, again in the language of the village people. "I am Grom, heir to the Wolkin throne, mate to Mellaia...son of Luna." He straightened. "The Winter King."

For a moment, the world was still and silent. Then the wind whipped snow around them.

Joffa tipped her head in respect. "Welcome, Grom, Winter King. We have been expecting you since the return of Luna's light to the temple. Will you hold council with us?"

Though Grom's expression showed he had many questions, he held them back.

For the moment.

"We will," he replied in his own language.

Mellaia chuckled at her grandmother's expression of shock.

* * * *

The walk to the village was less than reassuring. The looks of distrust and murmurs of the same ensured the entire Wolkin company was ill at ease.

They'd only taken half their guards with them, eight of the human/wariken teams. The rest had been left at the foot of the ramp. Their accompanying group was a force larger than the one who'd fought off the village warriors the night she and Grom mated, but it was smaller than the group Grom would have preferred to take with them.

Once they were settled in the council chambers—one human Wolkin and three of the wariken accompanying them, four of the village warriors doing the same, and the rest left outside—Mellaia introduced the other council members to Grom, and he gifted each an ear cuff.

Their amazement at the translation the cuff provided made Mellaia wonder how the Wolkin who'd come before had conversed with her ancestors. Perhaps the Wolkin who traveled to her world had learned the language, as she'd learned Wolkin on their world.

They settled in the traditional council circle, Groll on Mellaia's lap, Issah on Grom's, and Hareem on Joffa's. One wariken sat to Mellaia's left, another to Grom's right, separating them from the council members. The final one went to Hareem, laying down with his head in the babe's lap. The move prompted a squeal of delight from her son, and Mellaia smiled her encouragement.

Finally, discussions started in earnest.

Kaleeah, the eldest of the artisans, spoke first. "Why have you chosen to return here now?"

Something in her tone warned that this may have been a bad choice.

Though Grom had surely sensed it as well, he acted as if he hadn't. "We had an equitable trade arrangement with your people, which we lost for a time, due to catastrophe. We would like to reopen negotiations toward the same agreement we enjoyed earlier."

He didn't need to specify what that agreement was. The council members would know it.

Before Kaleeah could continue, Vardin, the strongest warrior, asked a question. "Why did you come?"

"I do not understand. Did I not just answer that question?"

Mellaia wondered the same.

Vardin shot a hard look at Mellaia, and Grom stiffened in response.

Her mate found his voice first. "Ask Mistress Joffa. It was her magic which called me to Mellaia. You must know we have never ventured this way at such a time before."

"So you claim it was chance that sent you here?"

"No," Mellaia offered less than patiently. "It was Luna's magic."

"Priestess nonsense."

Joffa glared at him, and the wariken guard lifted his head from her lap and snuffed in displeasure, showing his fangs.

To her surprise, Vardin jerked away, nearly leaving the circle. His hand crept to his weapon.

"Stop it," Mellaia ordered.

Vardin gaped at her. "The beast..."

"The wariken attacked when Grom came for me, *because* the warriors from the village attacked us. It was no secret I'd gone to summon my mate. Had your men *asked* Grom's purpose or inquired if I was in need of their protection, that battle would have been avoided."

No one spoke for a hand of tense moments, and Hareem's wariken guard settled his head again. Hareem yawned, then laid his head on the wariken's lush back, turning to settle for a nap on his new friend.

"Would I allow my son to sleep with a dangerous beast?" she continued.

That seemed to free Joffa's tongue. "Are all three — ?"

"Yes." Mellaia smiled. "Grom's people often have two babes at once. I... I suppose I am blessed to have three, though they sometimes try my patience."

Vardin found his voice again. "Will you take the ones you...changed with you when you go?"

Grom sighed. "If they wish to accompany us, but we will not force them to leave."

"Then you *knew* what would happen to them when you came here?" he accused.

Mellaia shook her head. "They learned by accident, by seeing what happened to me. At least... I *assume* the others who have been changed were similarly affected."

Joffa waved for silence. "Perhaps we should explain what happened after Mellaia's leaving. The Winter King can make a decision upon hearing it."

"How many were affected?" Grom asked.

"All those who were bitten but did not die from their injuries," she reported. "Those who were clawed suffered no effects from it. Four, in all. One was killed early on."

"So three remain," Mellaia whispered, her heart aching. She wanted to ask how many had been lost and who they were. *Not in this company. Tempers are already high.*

"Not here," Vardin snapped. "Take them or not, they are not welcome here."

"And if they return to the village?" Grom asked.

"They die."

"We will offer them safe passage and land of their own," Mellaia hastened to assure them.

Vardin scowled. "I hope—for their sakes—they agree to it."

More to come from Wolkin soon...

About the Author

Brenna Lyons wears many hats, sometimes all on the same day: former president of EPIC, author of more than 100 published works, owner of Fireborn Publishing, columnist, special needs teacher, wife, mother...and member in good standing of more than 60 writing advocacy groups.

Since she started publishing novel-length works in 2003, she's won 3 EPIC e-Book Awards (out of 16 finalists) and finaled for 3 PEARLS (including one Honorable Mention, second to NY Times Bestseller Angela Knight), 2 CAPAS, and a Dream Realm Award. She's also taken Spinetingler's Book of the Year for 2007.

Brenna writes in 26 established worlds plus stand-alones, poetry, articles and essays. She's a bestseller in indie/e fantasy and horror, straight genre and cross-genres thereof. Brenna has been termed "one of the most deviant erotic minds in the publishing world...not for the weak.' (Rachelle for Fallen Angels Reviews) Milieu-heavy dark work is practically Brenna's calling card, with or without the erotic content.

She teaches classes in everything from POV studies to advanced editing, networking to marketing. Brenna enjoys hearing from people who read her work and can be reached by e-mail.

Website: http://www.brennalyons.com/

Facebook: http://www.facebook.com/brenna.lyons

Email: brennalyons@FBP.comcastbiz.net

Also by this Author

Available from *Fireborn Publishing*

KEIF'S DEN AND PACK
Keif's Pack
Mother of the Keif
Keif's Den (Coming Soon)

PROPHECY
Prophecy: Revelations
Prophecy: Rapture
The Prophet's Mate
Prophecy: Rampage - Meet Gavin
Prophecy: Rampage (Coming Soon)

THE FANTASY CLUB
The Consort

WEREWOLF U
Werewolf U
Second Daughter
Alpha Son
Never Alone
Her Christmas Wolves
Werewolf U Stories (print)

RENEGADES SERIES
TYGERS
Renegade's Run (including *Max-Sec*)
Alpha House (Coming Soon)

URBAN GRIMM
Catch Me, If You Can
Three Wishes
Temptation of Eve
Put On Your Dancing Shoes (Coming Soon)

GRELLAN WAR
With Great Power
Playing With Fire (Coming Soon)
Jump Lover (Coming Soon)

BORN INVESTIGATORS SERIES
Hidden Away (Coming Soon)

Beyond the Veil
Fairy Wishes (Coming Soon)
Mine for the Night
Once in a Blue Moon
Overtime Pay
Stay With Me
The Fire God's Woman
The Punishment of Phoebus Apollo
Undead in Blue (Coming Soon)

Available from **Fireborn Publishing** in PRINT ONLY

NIGHT WARRIORS
Night Warriors
Will of the Stone
Bearing Armen
Hunter's Moon
Veriel's Tales I: Crossbearer Turned
Veriel's Tales II: Losing Regana
The Blutjagdfrau Chronicles

Bride Ball
Fire and Ice
Lovers' Kiss anthology
Monsters and Mayhem anthology
Paranormal Paramours anthology

Available from **Phaze Books**

ANGEL-WING SAGA
Sons of Heaven: Beldon

Blutjagdfrau Lost
The Warrior's Man
Damsel in Distress

STAR MAGES
The Master's Lover

XXAN WAR
Daahan Rising
Crossbred Son
Raashh Decisions

Enslaved
All I Want for Christmas is You
Fates Magic
All's Fair...
Black Sail
Mama's Tales
Dream Walk
Unexpected Daddy
Phaze in Verse
We Shall Live Again
May the Best Man Win
Nevermore
Marked
And It Was Good

Available from **Mundania Press**

STAR MAGES
Written in the Stars

Fairy Dreams
Monsters of Myth Anthology

Available from **Under the Moon**

Evil Overlords Union Issue #1 Anthology
Undead Embrace

"*Playing Games*" in *Forbidden Love: Bad Boys*
"*Marked*" in *Forbidden Love: Wicked Women*
"*The Master's Lover*" in *Forbidden Love: Sacred Bands*

Available from *Logical Lust*

"*Mine for the Night*" in *The Cougar Book* Anthology

Available from *Coming Together Charity Anthologies*

INSTINCT SERIES
"*Foundling*" in *Coming Together: Into the Light* Anthology

BORN INVESTIGATORS SERIES
"*Claim Mate*" (available separately and as part of the *Coming Together: Against the Odds* Anthology)

"*The Fire God's Woman*" in *Coming Together: Under Fire* Anthology

Available *self-published*

KEGIN SERIES
Earth-Born Lord
Graham: Training the Earth-Born Lord

NIGHT WARRIORS
Claiming a Lady
Stone Lord
Mother's Son

COLOR OF LOVE
A Safe Heart

Snapshots from a Poet's Life

Award-Winning Books

EPPIE/EPIC eBOOK AWARDS WINNERS
Coming Together: Against the Odds- 2010
Time Currents- 2010
Coming Together: Into the Light- 2011

EPPIE/EPIC eBOOK AWARDS FINALISTS
Fion's Daughter- 2004
Collected Poems: Book One- 2005 (now titled *Snapshots of a Poet's Life*)
Renegade's Run- 2005
Rites of Mating- 2006
All I Want for Christmas- 2006
Phaze in Verse- 2008
"The Fire God's Woman" in Coming Together: Under Fire- 2009
Three Wishes- 2010
Matchmaker's Misery- 2010
The Cougar Book- 2011
The Master's Lover- 2011
Bride Ball- 2011
Keif's Pack- 2016

DREAM REALM AWARDS FINALIST
Last Chance for Love- 2003

PEARL HONORABLE MENTION
Night Warriors- 2004

PEARL FINALISTS
Schente Night- 2003 (now included in *The Last of Fion's Daughters*)
König Cursebreakers- 2004 (now titled *Will of the Stone*)

JOYFULLY REVIEWED BEST BOOKS OF 2010
Written in the Stars- 2010

SPINETINGLER'S BOOK OF THE YEAR 2007

NOBODY: An Anthology of Dark Fiction- 2007 (Brenna's pieces of the anthology can be found in *Beyond the Veil*)

TRS's CAPA FINALISTS
Ultimate Warriors- 2004 (Brenna's portion is now available as *With Great Power*)
Written in the Stars

LOVE ROMANCE AND MORE CAFÉ BOOK OF THE YEAR RUNNER UP
Last Chance for Love- 2008

ROAD TO ROMANCE REVIEWERS' CHOICE AWARD
Prophecy: Revelations- 2004

LOVE ROMANCES REVIEWERS' CHOICE AWARD
Black Sail- 2003

ROMANCE JUNKIES BOOK CLUB STAFF PICK
TYGERS- 2003

FALLEN ANGELS ROMANCE RECOMMENDED READ
Devon's Price-2005 (now available in *Bearing Armen*)

JOYFULLY RECOMMENDED READ
Fairy Dreams- 2008
The Last of Fion's Daughters- 2009

TREBLE HEART FINALIST
Prophecy: Revelations- 2003